HOW
WINSTON
CAME HOME FOR
CHRISTMAS

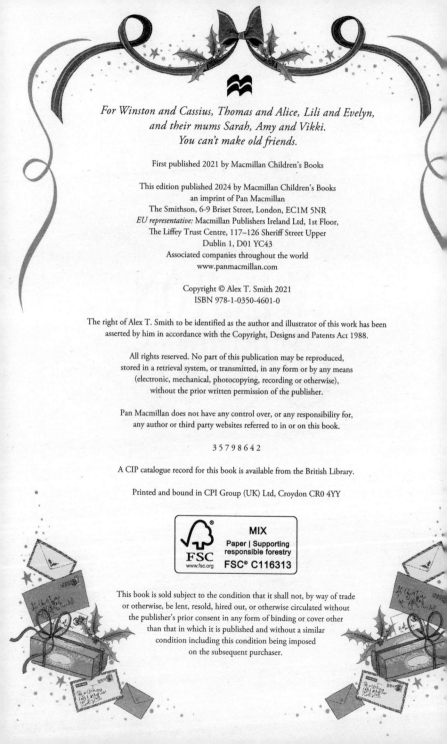

*For Winston and Cassius, Thomas and Alice, Lili and Evelyn,
and their mums Sarah, Amy and Vikki.
You can't make old friends.*

First published 2021 by Macmillan Children's Books

This edition published 2024 by Macmillan Children's Books
an imprint of Pan Macmillan
The Smithson, 6-9 Briset Street, London, EC1M 5NR
EU representative: Macmillan Publishers Ireland Ltd, 1st Floor,
The Liffey Trust Centre, 117–126 Sheriff Street Upper
Dublin 1, D01 YC43
Associated companies throughout the world
www.panmacmillan.com

Copyright © Alex T. Smith 2021
ISBN 978-1-0350-4601-0

The right of Alex T. Smith to be identified as the author and illustrator of this work has been
asserted by him in accordance with the Copyright, Designs and Patents Act 1988.

3 5 7 9 8 6 4 2

A CIP catalogue record for this book is available from the British Library.

Printed and bound in CPI Group (UK) Ltd, Croydon CR0 4YY

MIX
Paper | Supporting
responsible forestry
FSC
www.fsc.org
FSC® C116313

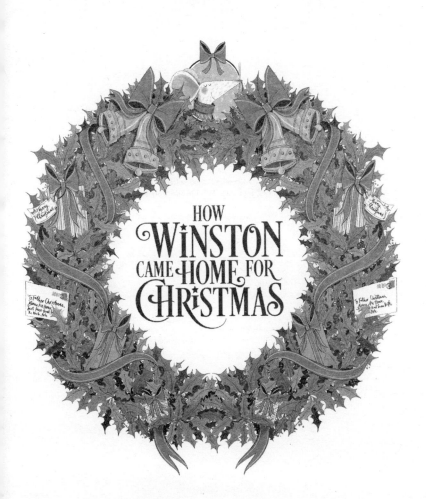

HOW
WiNSTON
CAME·HOME·FOR
CHRiSTMAS

Alex T. Smith

MACMILLAN CHILDREN'S BOOKS

How Winston Came Home for Christmas is a book written in 24½ chapters. You can read it as quickly as you want to (maybe even gobble it all up in one go!) or you can start reading it on the 1st of December, and then read one chapter a day in the run-up to the 25th, finishing with the ½ chapter at the end on Christmas Day itself. It could be fun to get cosy and read the story all by yourself, or you could share it with a grown-up. Maybe have a biscuit at the same time. Books and biscuits go so nicely together, I think.

Alex T Smith

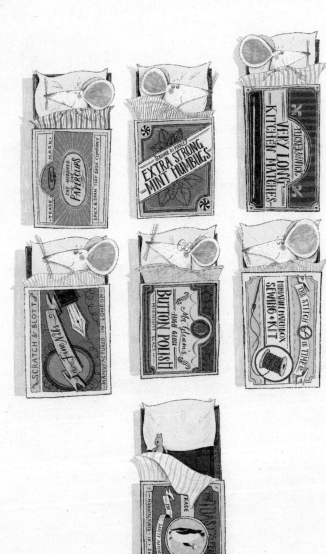

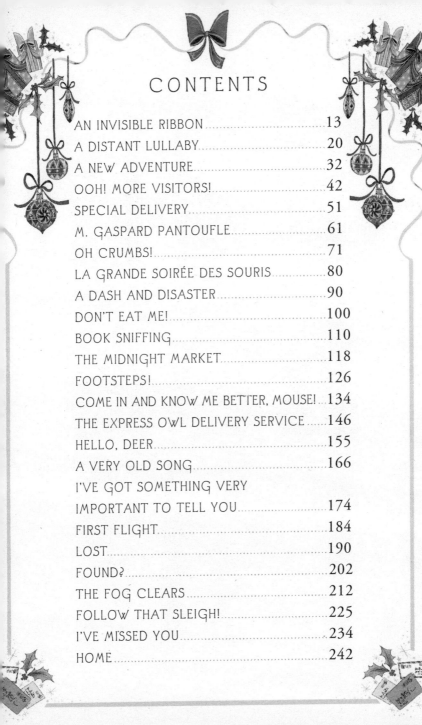

CONTENTS

AN INVISIBLE RIBBON

It was five days until Christmas and the snow had come. Soft and white, it covered the earth, making it shimmer and sparkle like the edges of a dream.

It was five days until Christmas and on the wide, open, snow-covered plains

someone was sneaking away from the herd, their hoofs crunching lightly on the powdery ground beneath them, their fur glittering and glowing like starlight.

It was five days until Christmas and high in the frozen sky great wings unfurled and flapped and soared in the falling snow. Bright yellow eyes blinked wide open, keeping a close watch on the world below.

It was five days until Christmas and the moon was shining, pearly and bright, through a high window on to a maze of dusty shelves. In the quietness, the only sound that could be heard was that of little footsteps pattering down the book-lined corridors.

It was five days until Christmas and in the frosty night air delicious smells wafted about like sorcerers' spells. In the shadows, two amber eyes opened, peeking out from their hiding place to check that the coast was clear. They wanted, more than anything, to step out from the dark and into the twinkling lights, but did they dare?

It was five days until Christmas and in dimly lit flour-dusted rooms, paws were washed thoroughly with soap and hot water, eggs were cracked, sugar was poured and ovens were lit . . .

It was five days until Christmas and in a room above the busy noise of a city someone walked round in a circle three times before settling down for the night. They closed their eyes, but after a moment a long lilac ear arched up into the air, shifting this way and that like a periscope, listening.

It was five days until Christmas and hidden amongst a tangle of ancient oak beams someone was waiting patiently. They allowed the cold winter wind to shiver around their wings. The view really was marvellous from up here in the rafters – especially as it was upside down.

It was five days until Christmas and in a dark and cluttered room someone was lying awake. They'd been awake for hours now. It was the same most nights, but something about this night in particular felt different. It was as if there was something magical in the air.

Carefully, they crept out
of their little bed
and slipped noiselessly
past a row of other
little beds. There were
seven of them, but only
six of them were being
slept in.

The figure tiptoed
carefully so as not to wake the
sleepers, then clambered up over
boxes in the flickering candlelight
until they reached a window.
They began to hum a little
song softly to themselves as
they looked at the crisp,
white, frozen world outside.

Something Very Important had been lost, and they knew for certain that it was out there somewhere. They hadn't known where to look before, but now they had a clue. Would it help them find what they were looking for?

It was five days until Christmas and a strand of winter magic was spiralling and twisting through the air. It was like an invisible ribbon that snaked and criss-crossed over the world, wrapping itself round each of the creatures in a neat bow, tying them together.

Nobody knew it yet, but the invisible ribbon was leading them somewhere. It was pulling them into a snow-covered Christmas adventure.

A DISTANT
LULLABY

It was five days until Christmas and in the snug attic bedroom high above the toy shop on Mistletoe Street a boy called Oliver was tucked up in bed. His face was washed, his pyjamas were on and the many blankets on his bed were pulled right up to his chin.

But he was not asleep.

A little torch was shining and Oliver's nose was stuck in a book. He was reading aloud in his best reading voice to a very small mouse who was perched on his shoulder. The mouse had large ears, a long tail, and was wearing a smart little jumper. His name was Winston and this was, he thought with a big, happy sigh, his Most and Very Favourite Time of the Day.

The shop downstairs was closed for the night, all was calm and quiet, and the two best friends were nibbling biscuits and cosily catching up on their exciting adventure story.

The book was terrifically thrilling and Winston found himself holding his breath as he listened to Oliver reading.

There were dramatic midnight dashes, a very curious mystery and a whole cast of extraordinary characters. Oliver and Winston were hooked.

Eventually, the chapter came to its cliffhanger end.

'Hmmm . . .' said Oliver, waggling his eyebrows, 'we could read the next chapter?' The two friends looked at each other before Oliver made a decision. 'No,' he said. 'We'll save it! It'll be more exciting that way!'

Winston nodded, and watched as Oliver put the book on his bedside table. Then the boy settled himself down to sleep, tickling Winston's ears to say goodnight. Usually, Winston would snuggle up next to him until he fell asleep, but tonight he had something busy to do downstairs. So instead he rubbed his tiny velvety nose against Oliver's, hugged his ear lobe tightly, then clambered carefully off the bed and scampered towards the stairs. At the door, he turned round to check. His best friend was already fast asleep and all Winston could see was a tumble of curly hair poking out above the blankets.

Stifling a yawn himself, Winston hurried quickly downstairs. It had been a very long day. But then, of course, it was five days until Christmas, so the toy shop had been extremely busy indeed.

How Winston had come to live in the toy shop had been an adventure and a half, which had taken place the previous Christmas. It had involved Daring Deeds, a LOT of snow, a midnight feast in a department store and even flying (and crashing) in a toy aeroplane.

But now all was safe and cosy. Winston had his enormous and lovely doll's house in the shop window in which to live, a human family who loved him and a Very Busy and Important job that he thoroughly enjoyed – Winston was the toy shop's Very Keen Helper-Outer, which meant he did all sorts of things that needed doing.

Today, he had scampered up to the highest shelves to fetch small toys, he had demonstrated the toy train that whizzed (puffing real steam) all around the shop and he had helped Oliver wrap up parcels by untangling the string.

He had also spent much of the day

supervising the post. This was his most favourite job. The shop sent lots of parcels all over the world and so boxes were always whizzing out of the door to faraway places. Winston checked them off the delivery list and he'd even taught himself how to work the typewriter by jumping on the keys, so that he could write the address labels himself. He'd also made sure that this year Oliver had written his letter to Father Christmas nice and early AND had posted it properly. Winston's whole adventure the year before had started with a troublesome letter that had stubbornly refused to stay put inside the letterbox.

Winston sighed happily. *Yes*, he thought, *I am a very contented little mouse.*

For a few minutes he gazed out of

the toy-shop window, while he waited for his friends, Pru and Eduardo, to arrive for their Once-a-week Late-night Second Dinner Club.

As Winston watched them, he felt a strange sensation suddenly wash over him. It was an empty sort of feeling, so he helped himself to one of the cheese biscuits he'd got out, ready for his friends to eat, and nibbled it thoughtfully. It was certainly very tasty, but after he'd finished it he still felt oddly empty.

He realized then that this feeling wasn't in his stomach, but in his chest, and it couldn't be fixed by eating something, no matter how delicious!

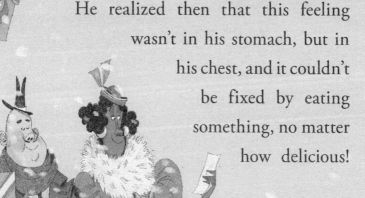

This was something else entirely. The odd thing was that this wasn't the first time that he had felt this strange feeling. Recently, the sensation had come over him whenever he had been watching the sorts of scenes that were currently going on outside the shop.

What did it mean? he wondered.

Just then, the large clock above the clockmaker's shop opposite chimed the hour and in the distance the cathedral bells began to ring. Nine bing-bongs for nine o'clock. Then the bells began to chime a tune. Winston stood up and smoothed down his jumper so he'd look smart when his friends arrived. As he did so, he found himself humming along, despite the fact that he didn't know the tune.

Except, he was surprised to discover, he did know it. Suddenly, as he stood there in the window, something strange and magical happened to Winston.

In his mind, he found himself hurtling backwards through his memories. Past the busy events of the day, past yesterday, past last week, past the last month, past the last year. Back, he continued, back before Oliver, back before being a street mouse.

Then, with a jolt, he stopped. In the strange, hazy world of his rememberings, he looked about. Everything was warmly lit and cosy, but it was also blurry, as if he was looking at it all through the wobbles of a jelly. He could make out a flickering light, and his ears waggled at the sound of someone humming. It was the gentle tune that the cathedral bells were playing.

But who was humming it?

Winston tried to remember, but the memory was very foggy. He could just about make out a shape. It was very unclear, but he could definitely see it. Or, rather, he could feel it. It felt full of kindness, and somehow familiar. He reached out to the figure, his heart drumming fast in his chest, and then:

Winston found himself back on the steps of his doll's house, blinking. He didn't know quite what had just happened, but he did know something.

He knew that somewhere, out there in the big wide world, there was someone Very Important to him.

And he knew that they were lost.

A NEW
ADVENTURE

A minute later, Winston's friends arrived. Lady Prudence Merryweather-Wiskerton the Third (but Pru to her friends) was a large fluffy cat with a sparkling diamond collar, and on her back was Eduardo, the most splendid rat in town. He lived in the food hall of the exclusive Fortesque's department store. Winston had met both of them on his Extremely Exciting Adventure last Christmas.

They found Winston blinking, and looking, as Pru said, 'like a kerfuffle in mouse form'.

'Brrr!' shivered Eduardo once Winston had opened the door and let them in. 'It's cold out there! Or it is, as the French would say, tres baguette!'

He smiled proudly, but Pru rolled her eyes. 'He's teaching himself French again,' she explained. 'Except he's getting it all wrong because he's learning it from the food packets at Fortesque's.' She peered at Winston closely over her whiskers. 'What's going on? You're quivering like a boysenberry blancmange!'

'The bells were chiming a tune,' whispered Winston. He was desperately trying to hold on to the memory, but it was slipping from him like satin ribbon through his paws. 'And all of a sudden I whooshed backwards in my head and remembered something from long ago that I had completely forgotten.' He described the scene as best he could.

'Someone is lost?' said Eduardo when he'd finished. 'Out there on Mistletoe Street?'

Winston nodded. Then he shook his head. Oh! It was all so confusing. 'Yes. No. I . . . I don't know,' he said. 'I don't know where they are!' He closed his eyes. The memories were there, but it was as if they were hidden behind a locked door and he didn't have the right key to open it.

'Well,' said Pru, primping her fur,

'you can count on us to keep our eyes and ears open, and if we even get a whisker-shake of a whisper that there is someone looking for a Winston we'll let you know.'

Winston shook his head. That strange emptiness squeezed round his chest again, but now it was joined by another sensation: the fizzing, bubbling feeling of an idea forming.

No, not an idea. A Plan.

He looked out at the moonlit street and nodded. 'I have to find them,' he said.

'But . . . but you don't know where they are!' squeaked Eduardo, flummoxed. 'Or who they are!'

'And what about Oliver?' said Pru.

Winston thought for a moment. Upstairs, fast asleep, was his best friend. As Winston thought of their nightly torchlit story times and of their top-secret treat tin, he felt a warm tingling feeling that made his toes wiggle. And yet . . .

He looked down at his chest, expecting to see a hole, shaped like the missing piece of a jigsaw puzzle. It wasn't really there, of course, but it felt as if it was, and he knew he had to find the piece that made him complete. That piece was whoever it was who he'd glimpsed in his memory.

'I have to know what all this means,' he said in a quiet but determined voice. Winston was, after all, a Mouse of Great Determination.

Pru and Eduardo nodded. This was obviously very important indeed, and if setting out to solve this Very Curious Mystery was what Winston needed to do, they would do everything they could to help him.

Winston got ready. He knew if he didn't leave immediately he might not leave at all. The toy shop was warm and safe, and whatever lay ahead might not be, but he had to go. He grabbed his trusty old scarf from the hook in the doll's house hall and dashed to the typewriter on the shop counter. Hopping about, he typed a note for Oliver to find in the morning.

```
I WILL COME BACK TO YOU.


             W

             x
```

Then he said, 'Ready!' and clambered with Eduardo on to Pru's back.

'Where are we going?' she asked.

Winston thought for a moment, then said, 'To the cathedral!' And off they went.

The cathedral was enormous, with a spire reaching high up into the tumbling snowflakes. The bells were no longer pealing, so the place was eerily silent as the three friends slipped through the heavy doors. Inside, the vast space glowed with thousands of candles, making the stained-glass windows glitter like treasure.

'You think whoever you saw in your memories might be here?' whispered Eduardo.

Winston didn't know. 'This was where the music came from, so it seems like a good place to start looking . . .' he said tentatively.

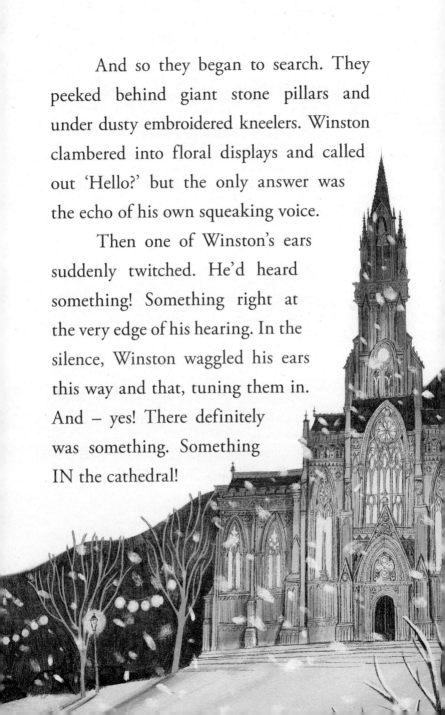

And so they began to search. They peeked behind giant stone pillars and under dusty embroidered kneelers. Winston clambered into floral displays and called out 'Hello?' but the only answer was the echo of his own squeaking voice.

Then one of Winston's ears suddenly twitched. He'd heard something! Something right at the very edge of his hearing. In the silence, Winston waggled his ears this way and that, tuning them in. And – yes! There definitely was something. Something IN the cathedral!

He scampered to the tower at the back of the church. The space was so tall that the ceiling disappeared into a worrying sort of gloom. Several thick velvet ropes dangled down in front of them, which, Pru explained, set the bells in the spire above ringing when you pulled on them.

'There's someone up there!' Winston said to his friends, pointing into the darkness.

'Ooh la la!' whispered Eduardo. 'It could be ghosts!'

Winston shivered. It could be, he thought, but it could also be the mysterious figure from his memory. He'd have to be brave and investigate. 'We need to get up there!' he said. 'Quickly!'

He didn't want to let whoever it was disappear.

'There'll be a staircase somewhere . . .' said Eduardo, but Winston was too giddy with excitement to wait. He clambered up on to one of the ropes and started to climb.

'Be careful!' cried Pru as Winston's paws slipped on the fabric. She leaped up to save him, but her claws got caught on the velvet rope. Winston managed to hold on, but as Pru waggled her paw she pulled the rope down sharply. This set the bell above them clanging dreadfully, then, with a sudden jerk, Pru managed to free herself, but – UH-OH! Disaster! Before she or Eduardo could stop it, the rope shot upwards and Winston, clinging on with all his might, whizzed along with it. He found himself hurtling, full speed, up into the darkness.

OOH! MORE
VISITORS!

The cathedral bells clanged wildly as Winston let go of the rope, bumping across the floor of the belfry and skidding to a stop in the corner of the room. He opened his eyes and found himself looking into an upside-down face.

The face grinned cheerfully and cried, 'Ooh! More visitors!'

Just then, Pru and Eduardo burst into the room having raced up the stairs to find Winston.

'Ooh! More visitors!' said the upside-down face again.

Winston shook his head to stop it from spinning and looked around properly to get his bearings. He was in a moonlit room at the top of the spire. Through the open windows he could see the whole city spread out, twinkling below.

Turning back, he found that the upside-down face belonged to an elderly bat who was dangling from a wooden beam. She fluttered down to help Winston to his feet as Pru and Eduardo padded over. When everyone was the right way up, Winston introduced himself and his friends.

'I'm Pamela Flittermouse,' said the bat as the bells stopped ringing. 'Have you come for a nice natter? You must meet my chums!' She swept a wing out in the direction of two creatures who were silhouetted against the moon, then said, 'Have you come for a natter? Oh no – I just asked that . . .'

Winston squinted at Pamela's friends, then grinned. He recognized the large pigeon and the tiny round robin.

'Edna! George!' he squeaked as Edna waddled forward and scooped Winston into her wings for a hug. Behind her, George was, as always, fast asleep. Winston had befriended the pair the previous Christmas when they'd helped him on his Very Important Mission.

'What are you doing up here?' asked Winston.

'We've come for a night-time natter with our old friend Pam,' said Edna. 'Considering she lives all the way up here, she always has the latest gossip. She sees everything that goes on.'

Pamela nodded. 'I always have the latest gossip. Oh! You just said that, didn't you, Edna?' She laughed, and Edna, Winston, Pru and Eduardo found themselves joining in too. Then, of course, Edna wanted to know what on earth Winston was doing in the belfry, having made such a dramatic arrival.

Winston told his friends about his Very Curious Mystery to find the figure from his memories. 'I thought perhaps they might have been up here, but it was your voices I heard,' he said. Then he had an idea. 'You don't know the name of the tune that the bells were playing, do you?'

Pamela shook her head. 'No – I said at the time that I didn't know it, didn't I, Edna?'

Edna nodded.

'Yes, I thought that's what I said . . .' said Pamela.

'Hmm . . .' considered Pru, 'a mysterious song . . .'

Eduardo stroked his chin ponderously. 'As the French say: une mysterious chocolat chaud . . .' Which, of course, isn't what they'd say at all.

Then Pamela said: 'And you can't remember anything else? Other than the tune and the blurry figure humming it?'

Winston shook his head.

'Maybe you should try listening to it again,' suggested Edna. And so Winston took a deep breath, shut his eyes and listened as Edna and Pamela hummed the tune.

In his mind, everything immediately went whooshing backwards like before. He was back in his rememberings again, with the same flickering light and the hazy figure humming to him, except this time they weren't humming. Winston realized that the tune, the lovely lilting melody that made him feel so warm and safe, was actually a song. It was a lullaby! But the words were in a language he didn't understand.

Then his nose wiggled. He could smell something. Delicious scents that smelt different to the cakes and biscuits the bakery on Mistletoe Street made.

Winston opened his eyes. A new language and delicious baking smells! These were new clues. He quickly told his friends what he'd remembered.

Everyone was terrifically excited, particularly Eduardo. 'Mangetout!' he exclaimed. 'I think I know what this means! They have the most delicious cake shops in the world in Paris – I wonder if you were born there?'

Winston gasped. Could that be true? Could he have been born in France?

It was then Pru's turn to get excited. 'I have a cousin,' she cried, 'well, a second cousin twice removed, actually, who lives in Paris! Right above a patisserie—'

'That means cake shop!' interrupted Eduardo who, for once, was correct.

'I know because when my people get letters from his people,' Pru continued, 'the envelopes smell divinely of bread and cakes! I'm sure my cousin Gaspard would help you with your search.'

Winston could hardly believe it! His heart soared, then just as quickly plummeted. There was a problem.

'How will I get to Paris?' he asked, whiskers drooping. He knew it was a long way away, and if he were to go by paw it would take for ever. Winston also knew that, no matter what, he HAD to be back with Oliver for Christmas morning. The thought of being so far away from him made a shiver of nerves shimmy up Winston's tail. He was an adventurous little mouse, but going to a whole other country was an entirely different matter.

Winston's eyes prickled, but he took a deep breath. He had to solve his Very Curious Mystery, and that meant being brave. He put his paws on his hips (to make him look braver than he felt) and concentrated on trying to think of a way to get to Paris, pronto.

Then there came a noise from the corner of the room.

SPECIAL
DELIVERY

It was George. He had been snoring (as always), but was now awake. He padded softly over to the group and yawned loudly. 'Want to get to Paris, eh?' he said sleepily.

Winston nodded.

'Hmmm . . .' said George. 'I think I might just have An Idea.'

Everyone leaned forward eagerly to listen.

'Why don't you post yourself?' George said, and then he sat back on his tail feathers and closed his eyes once more.

'Post myself?' squeaked Winston.

George opened an eye. 'Yes, that's the idea. Pop yourself in an envelope, get addressed to Pru's cousin, and then you'll be in Paris in an instant. The post is whizzing about like mad at the moment. It'll be far quicker than walking there – especially on those little paws!'

'Is that possible?' asked Eduardo.

'Can mice post themselves?' said Pru.

Winston didn't know, but he was

going to find out. His mind was racing. 'We'll have to go back to the toy shop,' he said. 'And I'll have to find an envelope and type a label and—'

He was interrupted by Edna. 'No! No!' she said. 'That will take far too much time. You'll have to go straight to the post office and sneak in there. They'll have everything you need – envelopes, stamps, that sort of thing.' She turned to Pamela. 'Pam? What time do the post trucks leave the post office?'

Pam grinned. 'I've just had a wonderful idea!' she said. 'Why doesn't young Winston post himself to Paris?'

Everyone looked at her.

'Oh!' she said with a giggle. 'Has someone already said that?'

Edna quickly went over the plan again. Thankfully Pam got it this time and she gave them the information they needed: the trucks set off from the post office at ten o'clock sharp.

Everyone squinted down at the clock on the nearby tower; they only had ten minutes to get Winston on his way to Paris!

Suddenly, there was a lot of action.

After saying a hurried goodbye and thank you to Edna, George and Pamela, Winston and Eduardo leaped on to Pru's back and she hurtled down the spiral stairs of the cathedral spire. It was dizzying and Winston felt a jumble of emotions:

excitement, anticipation, panic. He had to get on that post truck.

Pru burst out of the tower and shot like a fluffy white cannonball down the aisle, startling a choirmaster who'd come to tidy the cathedral in readiness for the morning.

She tumbled out on to the street and dashed through the crowds, weaving this way and that through the legs of people leaving restaurants and theatres. On her back, Eduardo and Winston clung on for dear life as they were bobbled about in the rush.

Eventually, they arrived at the post office, and not a moment too soon. Parked on the road outside, its engine belching great clouds of exhaust into the night air, was a truck. A man was already hurling enormous, well-stuffed sacks full of mail into the back of it.

'Quick!' squeaked Winston, and he and Eduardo dived off Pru's back, tumbling tail over ears until they crashed into the door of the post office.

With Pru acting as lookout on the street, the two rodent chums wiggled their way through the low letterbox and into the shop.

It was dark inside, but there was just enough light from a small, twinkling Christmas tree on the counter for them to see by.

Eduardo immediately rummaged around in drawers to find a suitably mouse-sized envelope, then Winston hopped on the typewriter to hammer out the address Pru had given him:

```
M. Gaspard Pantoufle
No. 804 Rue des Canelés
Paris
FRANCE


URGENT!
```

They stuck on as many stamps as they could find, to make absolutely sure it would get to its destination, before wiggling their way back outside, dragging the envelope with them.

'Hurry up!' mewed Pru. 'He's on his last few bags!'

The pile of sacks had diminished and only a couple remained on the pavement. Winston dived inside the envelope and Pru poked a few air holes in it with her claw. She was just about to lick the sticky edge shut when Winston realized that he would have to head off on this next part of his adventure alone – there was no room in the envelope for Eduardo or Pru.

It was a frightening thought. He was going out into the big wide world, by himself, to somewhere completely unknown, to find someone he only half remembered. Would he find the mysterious singer from his memories? Or would he get hopelessly lost, miles from his home and his friends?

Pru and Eduardo could tell that Winston was worried. Eduardo gave him a tight squeeze and Pru nuzzled him softly with her velvety nose. 'We will be waiting for you when you come back,' she said.

'Crème brûlée!' said Eduardo heartily. (He meant 'Bonne chance!', which means 'Good luck'.)

Winston giggled, feeling braver already. He nestled down inside his envelope while Pru stuck it shut and put it into the last mail sack.

Almost immediately, the bag was hurled into the lorry and the engine revved. With a final peek through one of the holes in his envelope, Winston saw his friends waving to him as he set off on his adventure into the night.

M. GASPARD
PANTOUFLE

It was a noisy, bumpy, uncomfortable sort of night. From inside his envelope, Winston heard the revving of the truck engine swap to the chug of a boat, then the huffing of a train. His belly was too jiggly with anticipation to really have a snooze, so he made himself as comfortable as possible and did some Big Thinking about his Very Curious Mystery.

The lovely sound of the lullaby was so clear to him now, but he still couldn't decipher the words well enough to know what language they actually were. And then there was the smell: delicious and exotic, yet homely at the same time. He squeezed his eyes shut for the five hundredth time to try to see the face of the creature singing to him. It was still impossibly foggy in his memories, but he had the very strong feeling that the mystery creature was a mouse.

Who are they? wondered Winston. Each time he thought of the song or the smell or even the hazy figure, his chest ached with yearning. How could he have forgotten something so important?

As dawn came, he found himself thinking about Oliver. 'He'll be waking up soon,' he said to himself, and he imagined his best friend reading the note he'd left. Winston hoped Oliver wouldn't be too sad. With any luck, they'd be back together very soon indeed, tucked up and sharing a cookie. Winston took another deep breath and concentrated on being brave.

Eventually, the train stopped and the mail sack in which Winston was hiding was on the move again. The envelope was sorted amongst the chatter of French voices (*Eduardo would love this!* Winston thought), and then he was in a postman's bag being swung through the streets of Paris on the delivery round. Winston peeked through the holes in the envelope at the morning revealing itself around him.

The air was sharp with frost and from every corner the most wonderful smells wafted about, reminding Winston that he'd missed both his second dinner last night and his breakfast that morning.

There was the buttery, flaky smell of croissants, the crunchy smell of baguettes and the squidgy whiff of cheeses. Rich, belly-hugging smells of onions and garlic mingled with hot, toasty chestnuts and Winston's little nose could hardly keep up with it all! None of the scents matched the one from his memories, but he enjoyed them immensely nevertheless.

Paris was as ready for Christmas as home had been. Lights twinkled and people were wrapped up against the cold wind that blew across the river. Their arms were piled high with parcels and heaped with mistletoe to hang above their front doors. Could whoever it was Winston was looking for really be somewhere amongst this glorious bustle?

As the postman's bag emptied around him, Winston couldn't help but wonder about what might lie ahead. What sort of cat would Pru's cousin Gaspard be? Pru could be Very Firm at times, but underneath it all she was as soft as her snow-white fur. But other cats weren't like that. Other cats had poking claws. Was Gaspard the sort of cat who would pat Winston around between his feline paws as if he was a ping-pong ball? That was a worrying thought indeed.

Presently, Winston's envelope was picked up, and he began to feel a bit wobbly with anticipation. He felt himself being slipped through a letterbox and landing with a bump on the floor. He heard paws approaching and loud sniffing, then the envelope was ripped open.

Winston gulped as a large paw reached in, and before he could scarper he was pulled out by his tail. He squeezed his eyes shut and prepared himself to be prodded with a claw.

But nothing happened.

Winston peeked through his eyelashes and found not the wide-open mouth of a hungry cat as he'd expected, but the smiling face of . . . a small, lilac-coloured poodle! A small, lilac-coloured poodle who smelt very strongly of floral perfume.

'Are . . . are you Gaspard?' Winston whispered. 'Pru's cousin?'

'*Oui! Oui!*' Gaspard nodded. He pulled himself up to his full height (which wasn't very high at all) and puffed out his fluffy chest.

'Well, I am Pru's SECOND cousin TWICE removed. But who—' He stopped to sniff Winston again in a friendly manner. 'Who are you?'

Winston explained to Gaspard why and how he'd travelled to Paris. Then he said, 'Pru thought you might be able to help me,' in a small voice.

Winston thought Gaspard might laugh at him – coming all this way to find someone he didn't even know did seem like a bonkers idea, after all – but, instead of laughing, Gaspard gasped and wagged his tail so hard and so fast he almost lifted off the ground.

'A quest!' he cried. 'An adventure! Oh, how I have longed for an adventure!' he giddily gabbled on. 'Every week my people take me to the hair salon to have my fur dyed and my claws painted. They make me wear my special coat and shoes there and back so I don't get grubby, and all the other dogs in the street laugh at me. But now: Excitement and Escapades! Baddies and Bandits! Daring Deeds! Danger!' He stopped, panting with glee. 'So tell me, *petit* Winston, what is our plan? I am at your service!' He saluted with a paw.

Winston rubbed his nose thoughtfully. 'Well . . .' he said, thinking that his task didn't really fit with his new friend's idea of an adventure. 'All I really need to do is have a look around a bakery. Pru said that there was one downstairs, and the mysterious mouse I'm looking for might be there!'

Far from being disappointed, Gaspard squeaked with excitement. There was indeed a bakery under Gaspard's apartment! It was where his owners bought him his breakfast croissants every morning.

Just then, Winston heard voices. Gaspard's humans were collecting the rest of the post! Gaspard quickly helped Winston into his velvet bed and hid him behind one of the silk cushions.

'It will be my pleasure to assist you!' whispered the poodle. 'But we shall have to begin our epic adventure tonight. Under the cover of darkness . . .'

OH CRUMBS!

Winston spent the rest of the day hiding out in Gaspard's bed. Well, hiding out is perhaps the wrong phrase. The bed was incredibly luxurious and so, feeling very tired from his long night journeying to Paris, Winston snuggled down among the velvets and silks and snored for the rest of the day. At supper time, Gaspard shared his dinner with his friend and Winston feasted on the most delicious food, freshly cooked by Gaspard's people.

Gaspard, however, was FAR too excited to concentrate on the food. Winston couldn't help but grin as he listened to Gaspard getting giddier and giddier as he planned how to break out of the apartment and into the patisserie downstairs later that night.

'THIS IS MY ADVENTURING DREAM!' Gaspard panted as his lilac curls bounced about in anticipation. Winston was also all of a jiggle at the thought of meeting the singing mouse and solving the

Very Curious Mystery in which he'd found himself mixed up.

Eventually, night fell and Gaspard's people went to bed. Gaspard, quivering with excitement, tiptoed down the hall with Winston on his back clinging to the poodle's soft, curly fur. Gaspard leaped up and opened the door before sneaking downstairs into the street.

Getting into the patisserie was a little trickier. Winston had to scamper all around its walls, crunching through the icy snow to see if he could find a way in. Gaspard kept watch, convinced that at any moment a gang of international spies or bandits would arrive. Thankfully, they didn't, and soon Winston had found a solution. At the back of the bakery a small window had been left a little open to let some of the heat from the ovens escape. The two adventurers managed to wiggle their way through, dropping with a bit of a bump on to the floor.

Inside, all was dark, but the light from the street lamp outside lent a warm, dim glow to the shop as Gaspard and Winston tiptoed about. The counter was full of the most delectable-looking treats: caramel-covered, cream-filled pastry balls were piled into tall Christmas-tree shapes, and chocolate yule logs sprinkled with icing-sugar snow sat next to rows of jewel-coloured macaroons that beckoned to be nibbled.

Winston walked around carefully, sniffing. The smells were delicious. None of them matched the scent from his memories, but at that particular moment it didn't matter. The enticing, sugary smell of the cakes danced about his whiskers, making him forget why he was there.

Luckily, Gaspard hadn't forgotten. He dashed about, searching and squinting into every dark corner. 'There isn't anyone here,' he said eventually, but the words were hardly out of his mouth when one of his long, lilac ears suddenly arched upwards like a submarine periscope. 'Wait a moment! There it is again!' he gasped. He clonked his head to the floor and listened. 'Every night this past week I have been hearing a strange noise. It's coming from down there!' His eyes were wide and wild. 'There is someone under here!' he whispered. 'You don't think it's bandits, do you?'

Winston didn't think that bandits crept about under the floorboards of cake shops, but he lowered his ear to the floor to listen anyway.

His ear wiggled – Gaspard was right! There was someone moving under there!

Together, Gaspard and Winston followed the noise through the quiet shop to behind the counter and watched in amazement as one of the floorboards lifted. Out popped a mouse carrying a large box wrapped with a bow.

For a moment everyone stood frozen, just looking at each other. Then Gaspard leaped into action. 'OH CRUMBS!' he cried. 'ARE YOU A BANDIT?'

The mouse, very chic in her little scarf and beret, looked offended. 'Moi, a bandit?' she sniffed. 'The very idea! I am Coco Gateaux, Madame President of the Guild of Mouse Bakers, Paris branch!' She eyeballed Winston. 'Are you here for the party?'

Winston shook his head. 'I'm . . . I'm looking for someone.' He explained to Coco what had brought him to Paris. He knew she wasn't the mouse he was looking for because his heart wasn't thumping in his chest. But he asked Coco if she knew other bakery mice.

'Well,' said Coco, 'as it so happens, I do know rather a lot of them. There are hundreds and hundreds of us in the city.'

Hundreds and hundreds of other bakery mice? Winston didn't know if he was delighted by this news or disappointed. How would he ever find the mysterious mouse before Christmas Eve if he had all those bakeries to investigate? It was only a few days away and he still had to get home to Oliver. 'Where will I start?' he asked, bewildered.

Coco grinned, her face crinkling up with joy. 'You are in luck, mon chéri! Tonight is the night of La Grande Soirée des Souris – the Great Mouse Party! The night each Christmas when we all come together from across Paris bringing our speciality cake with us –' she paused to gesture to the box she was carrying – 'and we eat and celebrate and dance. It is a wonderful evening and it is happening here tonight!'

Winston couldn't believe it. He felt jingly and jangly with excitement. 'Can I come with you?' he cried. 'And can my friend Gaspard come too?' He didn't want Gaspard to miss out on the fun.

Coco looked at Gaspard very carefully. 'Well,' she said, 'it really is meant to be only for mice . . .'

'Oh!' said Gaspard. 'I'm not a mouse, but, um . . . I do like cheese!' He waggled his eyebrows encouragingly.

'Ah! Perfect!' said Coco decisively. 'You are an Honorary Mouse for the evening. Now quickly, both of you – follow me. The party is about to begin!'

LA GRANDE
SOIRÉE DES SOURIS

The Great Mouse Party took place in a store cupboard at the back of the patisserie. Gaspard used his nose to open the heavy door, and Winston gasped at the sight that greeted him.

Bags of flour and sugar and gift boxes

for the macaroons had been pushed to the side and several of the floorboards lifted up to create a sunken dance floor. Strings of fairy lights glowed in loops and in the corner a band was playing jazzy Christmas songs on miniature, mouse-sized instruments. A fine sprinkling of icing sugar was falling from a flour shaker suspended high above the ballroom, and under it mice in their fanciest clothes twirled around, gossiping and squeaking with excitement.

And then there were the cakes! Set out in neat little rows were hundreds of parcels, each containing the most wonderful cakes and biscuits Winston had ever seen. He nearly lifted off his feet as he sniffed the scrumptious scent of raspberry, caramel, cinnamon and chocolate.

Next to him, Coco clapped her paws for quiet, and the band immediately stopped playing. 'Good evening, dear friends and colleagues,' she cried. 'It is with great pleasure that I welcome you to this year's ball.' Everyone cheered and clapped, but Coco held up a paw, shushing the room instantly again. 'Now, before our festivities can begin,' she continued, 'our new friend Winston here needs our help to solve a Very Curious Mystery. I want you all to listen very carefully!'

She gently pushed Winston to the front of the crowd.

Hundreds of faces looked up at him as he shyly explained why he was there. As he told them everything he could remember, the bakery mice of Paris crowded around him, eager to find out more and offer their advice. They were all very kind and friendly, but Winston didn't recognize any of them. He would know the mouse he was looking for when he found them because he would know them by heart.

'Perhaps some cake would help?' said a mouse with very pink cheeks. 'Cake is always good when you are trying to remember something!'

The mice agreed – cake of any kind was good for most problems, so Winston was presented with plate after plate of delectable treats to nibble.

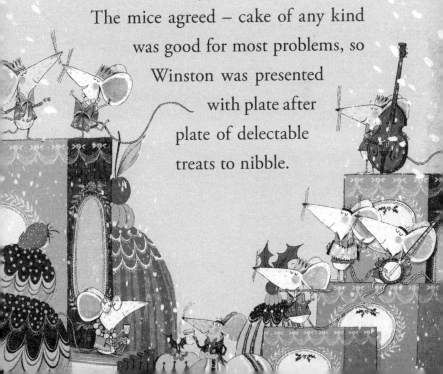

There were tiny fruit tarts and crunchy biscuits. There were wobbling puddings, and cakes made from what looked like thousands of thin layers of sponge cake and cream.

Winston dutifully nibbled at each one. They were all fabulous, but none of them transported him back to the strange candlelit room in his mind.

Eventually Coco took charge again. 'Enough!' she said. 'You all know that the best cake for remembering things are madeleines.' And with a great rustling of paper she unwrapped her own box and gave Winston one of the golden shell-shaped sponge cakes she'd made. She dipped it in a thimble of a lime-flavoured drink and handed it to Winston, who tucked in eagerly.

Whether it was the madeleine or the

rustling of paper that did it
Winston didn't know, but the
moment he squeezed his eyes shut,

he was suddenly back in his memories
once more.

He was surrounded again by the now
familiar flickering light of the candle, and
there was the delicious baking smell again.
But as his whiskers twitched he realized that

there were new smells in his memories.

'There's peppermint,' he muttered aloud, 'and . . . and a crispy dry smell . . . like paper.' Yes, it must be paper because there was the sound of rustling too. Then the gentle sound of the lullaby filled his ears. 'And there's the song again!' said Winston, still with his eyes closed, remembering. The music seemed to call to him, and the more he listened the more something became clear. 'I can hear the words properly this time!'

The Parisian mice shuffled closer to him.

Winston opened his eyes, blinking himself back from his memories and into the real world. All the bakery mice were looking at him expectantly.

'Well?' said Coco Gateaux.

But Winston shook his head. 'I can make out the words,' he said, 'but they aren't in any language I know of.'

Great twitterings and squeakings went through the crowd of mice. How Very Curious this Mystery was!

'You'll have to sing it to us,' said Coco. 'Us bakery mice have travelled all over the world. One of us might recognize the language.'

Everyone stood waiting for him to sing, but Winston suddenly felt shy again. The tip of his nose and his ears went bright pink. Gaspard, looking down on the scene, could see Winston needed a little bit of encouragement, so he leaned in and gave his tiny friend a nudge with his nose. It did make Winston feel better, and so he started to sing.

His little voice rang out around the near silent bakery.

When he was done, he saw all the mice were looking perplexed. None of them recognized the words Winston was singing.

'Can't you remember anything else?' someone asked. Winston squeezed his eyes shut once more and tried to remember. 'There's the music,' he said slowly, 'and the nice food smells and the sound of rustling and the smell of paper . . .'

He was about to open his eyes again when something changed. 'Wait!' he said,

and the mice surrounding him gathered closer still. Looking over the ballroom from the floor above, Gaspard dropped his head lower to get closer to the action.

As Winston listened to the song in his mind, his heart began to beat like a drum as a new feeling washed over him. It was warm and sweet like the madeleine. It felt safe, and like coming home.

The haze lifted and in his memory Winston looked into the face that was singing to him.

He opened his eyes. 'I know who is singing to me,' he whispered.

'Who?' gasped the mice, bustling closer.

Winston hardly dared to believe it, but he knew it was true. He took a deep breath.

'It's my mum.'

A DASH AND DISASTER

'You have a mum?' gasped Gaspard.

Winston nodded his head slowly. He felt all of a jumble again. He'd seen her kind, lovely face so clearly and had recognized it immediately. He'd known it by heart. But where WAS she? He knew –

just KNEW – she was out there somewhere.

The mice put their heads together. There were new clues now – the peppermint was a mystery, but the rustling paper sounds . . .

'Were you born in a bookshop?' asked a mouse, her large necklace of sugared almonds jangling in excitement. 'There's that lovely higgledy-piggledy one down by the river. I sneak in there for the recipe books . . .'

Winston certainly liked the sound of that, but the problem was the mysterious language. He just had a feeling – a strong feeling – that she wasn't from Paris.

A tiny mouse pushed his way to the front of the group. He was wearing large spectacles that kept sliding down his nose.

'Excuse me,' he squeaked, bowing politely. 'My name is Louis Mille-Feuille and I have a friend who lives in an enormous library with thousands of books in hundreds of languages. I think she could help you find the language your mum is singing!'

Winston's cheeks flushed pink with excitement. 'Is the library nearby?' he asked.

'Ah . . .' said Louis. 'Well, you see, the library is actually in Germany . . .'

Winston let out a tiny groan. Germany! That was a whole other country, and a big country at that! That meant another long journey – and he didn't have an envelope to ride in this time. How would he get there?

Everyone thought very hard, but it was Coco Gateaux who came up with a solution. 'This bakery is very famous and sends its macaroons all over the world. Look!' She pointed to the towering pile of macaroon gift boxes in the corner. They were mint green with swirly gold writing on them. 'We could pop you in one of those and send you straight to the library!'

'And,' added Louis, 'you could deliver some cake to my friend for me!'

Winston thought this was a marvellous idea. 'But will I make it to the post office before the post leaves?' he flustered.

'*Non!*' said a ginger-coloured mouse who worked in a patisserie near a post office. 'The post left hours ago, but you could always get the train. A big train loaded with goods leaves for Germany in about twenty minutes!'

Winston was in a tizz. How could he make the train if he had to run there in a giant box?

Suddenly Gaspard leaped to his feet. He flicked his ears back, stuck out his lilac chest, then said in a very grand voice, 'I WILL TAKE YOU!' His eyes were sparkling with the thrill of an adventure.

The mice cheered and set to work.

Within a few moments, Winston found himself tucked neatly into a macaroon box, which had been piled with cakes for the journey. An address was hastily written on top and then it was time to leave. He called his goodbyes from inside the box, and then Gaspard set off, out through the patisserie window and on to the streets. Gaspard ran as fast as his little lilac legs could take him.

Through the air holes poked into his box, Winston felt the chill of the icy air and heard the slushy snow splash as Gaspard raced through it.

His fur must be filthy, Winston thought, but he knew Gaspard wouldn't mind. This was what his friend had been dreaming of: a high-speed chase through the night.

Soon Gaspard bounded through the train-station doors and slid wildly across the polished floor, skidding and zigzagging through the crowds.

'There it is!' squeaked Winston, peering out from his box.

Gaspard ran towards the train, but as he did it started to pull away! Spotting that one of the doors was still slightly open, the poodle threw the macaroon box up into the air and then kicked it with his back paws, hurling the box towards the train. Winston twirled round and round before landing with a thud on top of a crate in the last carriage.

In the distance, Gaspard barked, *'Au revoir!'* his whole body fizzing with delight.

Winston carefully opened the box and stuck his head out to enjoy the crisp air streaming in from the gap in the door. All around him were crates filled to the brim with brown paper packages tied up with string. Winston marvelled at them all, thinking how each parcel had been picked and wrapped and sent to someone special who was cared about. Then suddenly his heart filled with wonder at the thought that he now had someone special who cared for him. Two, in fact! Oliver and his mum! Perhaps he had a whole family he didn't know about too!

Winston thought about this as he munched his way through the treats the mice had given him to snack on. Then, lulled by the rumbling motion of the train, he finally fell asleep.

The following morning, Winston awoke as the train pulled into a new station. The crate in which he was riding was lifted down and the parcels sorted into huge bags. Winston felt excited that he would soon solve his Very Curious Mystery.

Then disaster happened.

In the bustle of the station, someone bumped into the sack holding Winston's box. It fell over and parcels spilt out everywhere. A flustered man hurried to pick them up, but before he could grab the little macaroon box it was accidentally kicked and sent skidding across the busy station floor. It crashed into a shadowy corner by some bins and Winston tumbled out.

He started to panic. How would he get delivered to the library now?

Suddenly he heard something move behind him. He turned round and squeaked in alarm.

From the darkness, he was being watched by two beady amber eyes.

DON'T EAT ME!

The glowing amber eyes were joined by a long orange-and-black snout. Winston squeaked, stumbled on the slippery floor and fell backwards as the face of a fox loomed over him.

Winston and the fox looked at each

other for a moment and then, at the same time, they cried 'DON'T EAT ME!' and leaped away from each other.

It took Winston a moment to realize what had just happened. 'Me?' he said, too bewildered by the idea to be frightened. 'Eat you?'

The fox in the shadows looked at Winston from under a trembling paw. 'Yes,' he said, 'you might gobble me up!'

Winston couldn't help himself. He started to giggle. 'I won't gobble you up!' He laughed.

'Are you SURE?' asked the fox suspiciously.

Winston nodded. 'Absolutely sure. I don't think mice eat foxes.

I don't, anyway. I much prefer cake.' He picked up some of the spilt cake from his travelling box and held it out to share. The fox took it hungrily, but continued to look at Winston with large, worried eyes.

Winston tidied his scarf then stuck out a paw. 'I'm Winston,' he said.

The fox gingerly shook Winston's paw. 'I'm Heinz. Heinz Schmuddelig. If you aren't going to eat me, what are you doing here?'

Winston slumped down on the edge of the now crumpled macaroon box and told the fox everything. All about his journey from Mistletoe Street to Paris, then to Germany.

'You did ALL of that?' gasped Heinz. 'That's very brave!'

Winston wasn't sure if it was, really. 'Well, maybe,' he said. 'But you see I know I just have to solve my Very Curious Mystery. I'm hoping someone here will help me.' But, he thought sadly, that seemed a long way off now. The parcels from the train had long since vanished into the crowd and with it Winston's chance of being delivered to where he needed to be. He was completely lost.

'Well,' said Heinz, 'I think it's very brave. I wouldn't be able to do any of that. I'm . . . I'm not a very brave sort of fox. I live here behind these bins and only sneak out when people aren't looking. The world is a bit too big for me. Big and scary. And I worry about things a lot.'

Winston rubbed his nose for a moment, thinking. Heinz was obviously all alone in the world and Winston knew how that felt. Before he'd met Oliver, he'd also been all alone. Winston knew what it was like to sneak about in the shadows, because that had been his life too. But if his adventures had told him anything, it was that the world was big, yes, but it was also full of kindness. And especially at Christmas, when the air was full of magic.

Winston decided then that he wanted to help Heinz. He wanted to help him be braver and to see the magic fizzing around him. Suddenly, he had an idea.

'I need to find a library,' said Winston. 'I don't suppose you know where it is, do you? It's an enormous, old one, full of hundreds and hundreds of books.'

'Oh yes, I know where lots of places are,' said Heinz eagerly. 'Even though I haven't actually been to them. Look!' He pointed to the tatty cardboard box he slept in, under a blanket of crumpled maps dropped by people who visited the nearby tourist office. 'I study them when I can't sleep at night. They have all the important places in town on them. I can't read the words yet, but I CAN read the pictures.'

'Do you think you could take me to the library?' said Winston. 'And I can show you just how magical Christmas is on the way!'

Heinz didn't look very sure. 'We won't be gobbled up, will we?'

Winston put his paws on his hips and stood heroically. 'Fear not!' he cried. 'I will gobble up anyone who even THINKS about eating you! I promise!' And he crossed his heart and tried to look as brave and majestic as possible.

With cars hooting and people bustling about, Winston could see why Heinz could be frightened. But, just as he'd predicted, the air was also full of winter magic. It was much colder here than in Paris, and Winston was glad that he had Heinz's warm fur to nestle into. He sat up by his ears and kept leaning forward to reassure him and point things out to his new friend.

He showed him the sparkling ice on the branches of tall, decorated Christmas trees and how shop windows glowed like lanterns, painting the cold pavements outside with dazzling yellows and oranges.

As they waited to cross the road, Winston showed Heinz how to throw back his head to catch enormous fluffy snowflakes on his tongue. It wasn't long before Winston noticed that a sparkle had crept into his eye. 'See,' he said, 'magic is everywhere – you just have to look for it!'

As the night set in, the city began to twinkle with thousands of new flickering lights.

'We're almost there, I think,' said Heinz. They turned the corner and found themselves in a wide square, across which the library loomed. But the square was far from empty. Winston's whiskers wobbled and his belly rumbled as he sniffed the hundreds of smells sizzling in the air from the enormous market in front of him.

Winston was just about to suggest they took a little, tiny trip to look at some of the stalls and maybe have a little, tiny nibble of some food, when a movement caught his eye. A bemittened woman was standing at the half-open library door, fumbling in her handbag for a key.

'Oh no!' cried Heinz. 'She's shutting the place up!' The door seemed to be the only entrance – if it got locked up tight, the answer to Winston's Very Curious Mystery would be locked up inside with it!

'We have to get in,' said Winston. 'But how?'

Just then a crowd of children playing in the snow tumbled into view. They were in very giddy spirits and Winston watched as one of them – a cheeky-faced scallywag – rolled up a snowball and hurled it at the library. It splatted against the door just above the librarian's head. She spun round and frowned sternly.

Her eyes narrowed.

The children stopped still and held their breaths. Winston held his, too. The children were in for a terrific telling-off – he just knew it.

But then, to everyone's surprise, the librarian grinned. She swooped down, scrambled about in the snow and made a gigantic snowball of her own. The open door to the library behind her was quite forgotten as she patted her icy grenade and took aim.

'Quick!' squeaked Winston, and like a flash Heinz dashed through the door, just as the librarian fired her snowy missile at the hooting children.

A moment later the door closed with a heavy clunk, and Heinz and Winston found themselves locked inside the deserted library.

BOOK SNIFFING

Winston and Heinz scampered up the wide marble steps and into the main reading room. It was imposing but warm, and in the very centre was a Christmas tree, though it was unlike any Winston had ever seen before.

It was made entirely from books, with hundreds of twinkling lights nestled among them, and was decorated with dangling bookmarks. Around it, disappearing off in all directions, were towering corridors of bookcases, all heaving with giant tomes.

Heinz looked around in amazement. 'And in each of these books is a story?' he whispered.

Winston nodded. 'Well, almost every book,' he said, and he explained that some books had facts in them instead. He hoped at least one might help solve the mystery of the language his mum was singing in his memories.

'I would like stories best,' said Heinz, considering it all very carefully.

Winston agreed. 'The nice thing

about stories is that you can go on all sorts of exciting adventures without actually leaving your armchair or bed,' he said, and for a moment he thought about Oliver back home in Mistletoe Street reading their book by himself. Then a slightly worrying thought appeared – time was running out. Winston had promised to get back for Christmas morning and that was getting closer every second, but he still didn't know where his mum was. That funny aching feeling in his chest came again at the thought of never finding her.

Just then there came a strange clonking noise from somewhere nearby. Heinz's eyes grew wide with alarm. 'Monster footsteps?' he said. 'Monsters who gobble up foxes?'

Winston shook his head. Definitely

not that, but what was it? Gently, he led Heinz through the mazes of bookshelves until they discovered the source of the noise.

Sitting at a high desk, illuminated by a single lamp, was a rat with a shawl draped about her shoulders. She was busily fussing with books and stamping a sheet of paper with a heavy-looking stamp.

Winston and Heinz scurried closer and saw that in front of her was a little sign that said:

INGRID LESERATTE
NIGHT LIBRARIAN

Winston's ears waggled excitedly – he'd found the creature who might be able to help him!

'If you have come for a book,' said Ingrid, peering at them, 'you'll have to wait a moment. Goodness me – so many to sort this evening.' She gestured to the wobbly towers of books surrounding her.

'Can we help you?' asked Winston.

Ingrid stopped her stamping. 'Yes,' she said, 'that would be most kind. You look like a good strong pair.'

For the next half an hour, Winston helped Ingrid check the books and stamp

ZURÜCKGEGEBEN

against the titles on her list. Then it was Heinz's job to carry each book gently in his mouth and carefully put them back in the right place.

'Thank you so much,' said Ingrid when they'd finished. 'That job usually takes me all night on my own.' She poured them each a thimble of lingonberry juice, and Winston introduced himself and Heinz. Then he remembered the cakes Louis had given him in Paris to pass on to his friend. He pulled the parcel from under his jumper and presented them. They were more than a little bit squished, but Ingrid didn't seem to mind. She kindly shared them out.

'Dear Louis – such a sweet boy,' she said, tucking in. 'Now, you've helped me, so how can I help you?'

Winston explained that the mice in Paris had thought that Ingrid might be able to help him identify the language of the lullaby. Under the glow of the bookish

Christmas tree, Winston tentatively sang the mysterious words.

Ingrid listened carefully. 'Hmmm . . .' she said. 'Now that does sound similar to quite a few languages I can think of, yet it is also entirely different. There's only one thing for it: if in doubt, consult a book! Follow me!'

And so Winston and Heinz pattered softly through the library after Ingrid as she led them to a dusty corner. She started to pull books from the shelves and flick through them. 'This is the Language section,' she explained. 'These are all books about words.' Winston had always loved words. He remembered tracing them with his paw on the newspapers he slept under when he couldn't sleep.

As they searched through the books, Ingrid twittered away to herself, thinking of new ideas when her previous investigations hadn't proved successful. 'There must be something to help here!' she said, pulling another thick tome from the shelf.

But eventually she shook her head, sighing. 'I can't find any answers anywhere.'

Winston's ears drooped and Heinz patted his little friend on the head with a paw to comfort him. Ingrid, however, pulled her shawl tightly round her shoulders and looked determined.

'But I know someone who might be able to help us,' she said. 'It will involve a trip to the Midnight Market.'

THE MIDNIGHT MARKET

Squeezing through a rattling, ill-fitting window at the side of the library, Ingrid led Winston and Heinz back out into the market that filled the square. Snow was falling in sheets, and through the dancing flakes lights sparkled and glowed like jewels. Crowds of people were laughing and nattering, eating and buying food and gifts from the stalls. Somewhere at the centre, around the enormous Christmas tree, a band was tooting and parping through a selection of famous carols. The whole place felt like a gigantic Christmas party.

Heinz trotted carefully through the crowds so as not to be spotted, but Winston marvelled at how much braver the fox was after such a short time.

'My friend will be here somewhere,' said Ingrid, nosing about. 'She likes good food and at Christmas there is nowhere better for a midnight snack than this market. The traders have come from all over the world and have brought with them the most delicious treats.'

After a few minutes, Winston thought that if he had to go past one more stall without eating something his belly would roar like a lion and his head would fall off. He knew he had his Very Curious Mystery to investigate, but at that very moment he thought he'd better deal with his Very Grumbling Belly first. So the three friends decided to have a look and a nibble at each of the stalls.

'Who knows?' said Winston. 'There might be a clue at any one of them!'

They visited the stalls one by one. There were great slabs of fruity stollen, chunks of marzipan and towers of squidgy nougat. There were boxes of sugared mice, and sweets that looked like gemstones. Great vats of bubbling stews set Winston's nose all of a tremble, and bowls of hot purple borscht soup smelt earthy and delicious.

The three friends nibbled on golden pillow-like dumplings called pierogi from the Polish stall, and chomped their way through mounds of sticky baklava from Greece, buttery panettone from Italy, and rich, fruity Christmas pudding from England.

At each stall, Winston waggled his ears to listen. Surely someone must be speaking the same language as his mum? But, as hard as he listened, he just couldn't find anyone who sounded like her.

As Heinz and Ingrid, who were getting on fabulously well, inspected some stalls surrounding a glittering ice sculpture, Winston stopped and sighed. He felt that every time he thought he was close to solving his Very Curious Mystery the

answers continued to be just out of reach.

'If only I could remember what the words of the lullaby mean,' he said to himself. Something really extraordinary must have happened for such an important thing to have disappeared from his head. He shivered, despite the fact that he was warm from eating all the hot food. All around him people were huddled together, having a lovely time. It was like looking out of the toy-shop window at the families enjoying themselves again, and that funny hungry feeling grumbled in his chest.

Suddenly he felt a little bit homesick, not just for Oliver and his Mistletoe Street family and friends, but also for his mum. She looked so kind and lovely in his memories, just how a hug would look if it came to life in the form of a mouse.

Oh, where IS she? he thought. *And will she remember me if I find her?* The market continued to bustle about him, but Winston sat down on a dropped pretzel to think.

Then his nose twitched.

Nearby, there was a smell of baking that seemed almost familiar. It wasn't quite the smell he remembered, but it was close. It smelt, he realized, gingery and peppery, and certainly very scrumptious. Leaping to his feet, he scampered off to find it.

Round the corner was a stall selling rich, dark gingerbread. Behind the overflowing wooden crates and the gingerbread reindeer-shaped biscuits, a couple, well-togged against the chilly night in colourful embroidered clothes, were chatting. Winston waggled his ears. It wasn't the language he was looking for, but it was the closest thing he'd heard so far.

Quickly he turned and ran back through the market, darting round and over and through large feet, scurrying over the frozen ground to find Heinz and Ingrid.

He discovered them inspecting an enormous stall that groaned under mountains of cheese. There was every sort you could imagine. A huge pot was bubbling away deliciously, and beside it large wheels of cheese wrapped in brightly coloured wax jackets sat next to wedges so big Winston could have hollowed them out and lived inside them. This was an exciting thought, but the little mouse shook it from his head – now was not the time. He had something important to tell his friends.

He gabbled at high speed about the new clue. 'What shall we do?' he asked urgently.

Ingrid considered for a moment, then something behind Winston's head caught her eye. She grinned. 'Not a moment too soon!' she said. Then she turned back to Winston and Heinz. 'I believe that my friend is over there, wrestling a sausage, and if ANYONE can help us, it's her.' And, bustling away importantly, she led Winston and Heinz over to the enormous, shimmering Christmas tree.

FOOTSTEPS!

Winston was not the only creature in the city on a Most Important Quest.

Not too far away, *another* mouse scurried down a snow-covered side street, their paws slipping on the icy cobbles. Every bit of their little body felt tired and cold.

It had been a long few days with many, many miles covered, from the back of a bird to the rattling, freezing carriage of a night train thundering through the countryside, searching all the time for clues and never knowing if they were going in quite the right direction.

Lots of large human feet were now crunching through the snow around them, and weaving among them was exhausting work. The mouse took a moment to sit on a step and catch their breath, but no sooner had they stopped when their stomach grumbled loudly and they realized they were famished. They still had a few dwindling supplies from home in their bag, of course, but they really wanted something more substantial, more filling. More delicious.

At that moment, the wind changed. It shivered round the corner and down the street, blowing a fine powder of fresh snow from window ledges and the bare branches of trees. The breeze brought with it a most tantalizing smell that made the mouse waggle their nose, their whiskers twitching this way and that.

Food! they thought, *and lots of it!* Delicious, wonderful food, the different smells tumbling all over each other in a great wave of belly-busting loveliness.

Where was it coming from? They followed their twitching nose towards the source of the scrumptiousness. Down the street they pattered, sweeping round the curve of an imposing library building on the corner, and then out into a vast and glowing market square.

The little mouse's eyes widened as they wandered among the full-to-bursting stalls, stopping here and there to try a nibble of this and a pawful of that. Soon the mouse started to feel better, and much warmer too, so they stopped their busy scurrying and took a moment to take in the scene around them. There was the large and beautifully decorated Christmas tree in the centre of the market, glistening ice sculptures and the cheerful noise of people enjoying themselves.

The mouse then looked down and saw that the frozen ground was embroidered with hundreds and hundreds of footprints, big and small, zigzagging all over the place, making intricate patterns in the snow.

Then they spotted something very interesting indeed.

Tiny footprints. Pawprints, in fact. Tiny pawprints not dissimilar to their own. These ones seemed to come from a stall selling gingerbread, a smell that was so familiar yet ever so slightly different.

Where were these tiny pawprints going? And who had made them? Could there perhaps be another creature here who could help with their Most Important Quest?

The mouse began to follow the footprints through the snow. Down a row of stalls they went, and as they crept carefully amongst the human feet, their whiskers wobbled again and their pink nose twitched delightedly. Cheese! Somewhere nearby there was cheese! And the tiny pawprints were going towards it!

The mouse quickened their pace, hurrying to the end of another stall, and turned the corner. Then they saw it. In the distance between a jumble of human legs and feet, and silhouetted against the bright glow of a large lantern, was the maker of the pawprints.

The mouse felt their heart beat fast with excitement. Another mouse! They were just about to run as fast as they could towards the stranger when something stopped them in their tracks.

The mouse in the distance was standing at the groaning cheese stall, but

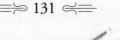

he wasn't alone. There was a rat there, wrapped up in a shawl, and, more worryingly, the large, orange, unmistakeable form of a fox!

The excitement the mouse had felt turned to paw-wringing worry. They darted back out of view and stood with their back pressed hard against the rough wooden side of a stall. They hardly dared to breathe in case the fox sniffed them out.

One minute passed.

Then another.

Then the little mouse slowly braved a peek back round the corner. The fox had gone, but so had the other mouse and the rat.

For a moment the mouse dithered about going to the stall and getting some of the cheese, but eventually decided against it. The fox could still be there, lurking about. So instead the mouse took a deep breath and turned the other way.

Then she continued on her journey, all by herself again.

COME IN
AND KNOW ME
BETTER, MOUSE!

Ingrid's friend was a tawny owl named Hilda Klappenflügel, who had set up home for a few days in the large Christmas tree in the centre of the market square. She was wearing a rather extraordinary-looking hat she'd fashioned

from a dropped Christmas decoration. She'd had a few glugs of the warm spicy drinks available in the market and was now wildly in the festive spirit. She was also, Winston was delighted to discover, absolutely not the sort of owl who would nibble on mice.

'Why would I do that?' she boomed in her loud, hearty voice. 'Heaps of tastier grub here! Anyone want a sausage?' She waggled one about with her foot, but her guests declined. 'Now, come in! Come in! And know me better . . . er . . . mouse!' And she ushered them in under the tree out of the snow.

Ingrid explained that although Hilda travelled a lot she always stopped by the library to pick up a good read and to

have a natter with the night librarian whenever she was in town. Once Hilda had even stayed in the library for a few days.

'Absolutely FILTHY weather it was,' said Hilda. 'But dear Ingrid here insisted I stay with her so she made me a bed on one of the shelves in the Ornithology department.

Can't remember the last time I was so snug. And I read simply PILES of books, didn't I, Ing? There was that fantastic one about—' But, before she could start reminiscing, Ingrid interrupted her friend to introduce Winston and Heinz, and told the owl a little about Winston's quest.

Hilda listened and then peered intently at Winston with her large yellow eyes. 'Hmmmm,' she said, 'YOU'RE the adventurous mouse? I'd heard chatter about a mouse scampering all over the place on some sort of quest. Terribly brave for such a little thing like you to do on your own.'

'Oh, I haven't been on my own, really,' said Winston. 'Everyone's been very kind and helpful.'

'And that is why we are here,' said

Ingrid. 'We think you might be able to help Winston with his Very Curious Mystery.'

At the word 'mystery', Hilda dropped the mince pie she was just about to gulp down and fluffed her feathers up excitedly. 'Mystery!' she cried. 'Oh, I simply adore mysteries! Do you remember that mystery book you loaned me, Ing? The one with the train that got stuck in the snow and that funny little detective who had to—'

Ingrid interrupted her friend. 'Yes, yes,' she said quickly. 'Of course! Now, do listen carefully, Hilda, while Winston tells you his puzzle.'

And so Winston told his tale. He started at the beginning, from hearing the bells on Mistletoe Street, all the way to meeting Heinz and exploring the library

with Ingrid. He explained about the smells that he remembered every time he went back into his memories: the peppermint and the dry, rustly paper scents, and the smell of cooking, and how in the market there was that tantalizingly similar (but not quite right) whiff. Then, of course, there was the lullaby.

With Heinz's encouragement, Winston closed his eyes and sang the strange words again. Every time he sang them, he felt as if there was a ribbon tied round him that was connecting him to his mum. She felt closer now.

Hilda listened carefully.

'Do you recognize my mum's language?' asked Winston. 'It sounds similar to the one at the gingersnap stall.'

'Most interesting,' said Hilda thoughtfully. 'That's Swedish you heard. It does sound rather like your lullaby, but it isn't quite right, is it?'

Winston shook his head.

'I must think about this,' said Hilda, and she closed her eyes. She closed her eyes for a long time. So long, in fact, that everyone thought she might have gone to sleep.

Eventually Ingrid prodded her. 'Well?' she said. 'What do you think?'

Hilda jumped, yelled, 'SCHNITZEL!' while looking a bit confused, then remembered what Ingrid was talking about. 'Oh yes!' she hooted. 'Our mystery! Well, my thinking is that young Winston here is definitely from somewhere Up North. Sweden? Norway, perhaps? The only thing for it is to go and do some detective work. Someone up there will know.'

Winston's heart started to drum fast. 'How can I get to Sweden?' he asked, his mind whirring. He counted on his paw to work out what day it was. Christmas Eve would soon be here and, whatever happened, he had to get home for Christmas. Poor Oliver would be missing him and he couldn't break his promise. Time was running out. There must be a way to travel to Sweden quickly.

Luckily, Hilda came to the rescue. 'I will take you!' she said grandly.

'You will?' said Winston, all goggly with amazement. 'You mean we'll fly?'

Hilda nodded.

'Are you sure?' asked Ingrid. 'That's

an awfully long way and you aren't as young as you were, Hilda.'

Hilda dismissed this. 'Nonsense!' she said. 'Give me a chance to dust off the old wings a bit. We'll find your mum in no time!'

Winston couldn't believe it. The last time he'd tried flying he'd had that unfortunate incident involving a toy plane and a blizzard, but he could be just hours away from finding his mum! He knew he'd have to risk it.

He nodded, said, 'Let's go!' and he and Hilda started to get ready.

Then Winston had a thought. 'Wait!' he said. 'What about you, Heinz? Where will you go?' Winston didn't want his friend going back to that cold corner of the train station behind the bins.

But before Heinz could open his mouth Ingrid patted him kindly on the paw. 'Oh! He's coming with me!' she said firmly. 'Back to live in the library. I know a nice warm place where he can sleep undisturbed, and in the evenings he can help me with my tidying. I could do with some extra paws about the place.'

Heinz beamed.

'And I'm going to teach you to read too!' said Ingrid. 'We'll start in the Children's Books section. Everyone knows that's where all the best stories are.' At this news Heinz threw himself backwards into the snow and wiggled about excitedly.

It was then time for goodbyes. Winston hugged his new friends and promised to write to them when he got back to Mistletoe Street.

'And I'll be able to read it myself!' said Heinz with a grin.

Winston hopped on to Hilda's back. She straightened her hat, unfurled her wings, and with a short run and a leap she launched herself into the air, and Winston watched the market and his friends disappear into the snow behind him.

THE EXPRESS
OWL DELIVERY
SERVICE

The flight was like nothing Winston had experienced before. The last time he'd flown he'd been terrified, but this . . . this was extraordinary.

Hilda's wings beat against the cold winter air as they soared through the night.

They flew over sparkling towns and wide, white-blanketed fields. They swept over steep, dark, pine forests dotted with snow-covered castles that looked as if they'd been spun from sugar and dusted with diamonds. They swooped down past tiny houses on little islands in the fjords, where Winston peeked in at cosy candlelit rooms.

Mid-flight, Hilda hollered over her shoulder that she knew lots of creatures who could help them, and Winston soon discovered that she hadn't been fibbing. It was as dawn broke that their detective work really got underway. Their first stop was deep in a forest with a couple of sleepy-faced red squirrels who lived in the trunk of a large tree. They had decorated it beautifully with mistletoe.

'Sorry to wake you,' Hilda said, 'but this is frightfully important.'

Winston told them about his Very Curious Mystery and, with Hilda's encouragement, he sang them the lullaby. They didn't know it, but they did have an idea.

'You COULD try Benny?' said one squirrel. 'He's always wandering about picking up news and information.'

'And if you ARE going to see him,' said the other squirrel, 'would you mind giving him this from us?' He handed Winston a parcel, neatly wrapped up and tied with string.

Benny was a large elk. They found him in a clearing where he was struggling to get a string of little festive lanterns untangled

so he could hang them about his antlers. Winston leaped to help and soon he was looking resplendent. He delivered the squirrel's parcel to him then he listened in his large, gentle elk-y way to his story. He thought the song sounded like it could come from further north.

'There's something about it that makes me think of icicles tinkling,' he said.

Hilda waggled her eyebrows at this. 'Another clue, dear Winston!' she said.

Benny suggested that they try his friend Anni-Frid, who had, he said, the most wonderful singing voice. Benny thought she might recognize the song.

And so they set off, once again with a new parcel to deliver.

They heard Anni-Frid before they

spotted her. At the top of a frost-covered dam in a large river a beaver was singing loudly and fussing with a wreath she'd made from pine cones. She'd heard of a little mouse travelling across the country to find someone lost and was very glad to meet Winston. She didn't know the song, but suggested a whole list of animals who might be able to help.

Winston and Hilda spent the rest of the day zigzagging back and forth across the country delivering gifts and trying to find more clues.

'We will find your mum,' said Hilda as evening set in. 'I promise.'

Winston nodded his head enthusiastically, but inside he was a jumble of worries.

He was worried about his mum and whether he would ever find her. He worried about what had happened to make him forget all about her and then he worried about Oliver, or, more specifically, about the post. It was inevitable that his head should turn to the post, with him and Hilda acting as an express delivery service.

I hope Oliver is remembering to get all the parcels ready properly, thought

Winston. There would be so much to do this close to Christmas, and he hoped Oliver was managing without him to stick the stamps and tie the strings and—

'BIT BLIZZARDY!' came Hilda's booming voice suddenly.

Winston blinked and looked about. He'd been so lost in thought he hadn't realized that it was dark and the snow, so gentle earlier, was now a great blizzard all around them.

'We'll have to stop!' called Winston, and Hilda nodded.

'I'LL LOOK FOR A TREE!' she hooted, but she didn't need to look far because – YIKES! – one suddenly loomed out of the swirling snow in front of them. Hilda swerved, but clipped her wing on a branch.

Winston slipped. He scrambled to stay on Hilda's back, but her feathers were damp and his paws were tiny and slippery. He tumbled from her shoulders. He bounced and boinged and whacked and thudded on hundreds of spiky branches before landing with a hard FLUMP in the snow below.

HELLO, DEER

W inston's head was buzzing from his tumble and his ears were packed full of ice.

He slowly sat up in the deep, cold hole he'd made in the snow and clambered out, shaking his head as he did so. He was in a small clearing in a little clump of trees. Everything was white and frozen, and the falling snow made it all silent and still and strange.

There was no sign of Hilda, so he began to tiptoe about, slowly trying to find anything that would tell him either where he was or the whereabouts of his friend. Suddenly he bumped into a tree branch.

Except the branch cried, 'EEEK! WHO'S THERE?' and dived for cover.

It was then Winston realized he hadn't walked into a tree at all. The branch was, in fact, a leg! It belonged to a small reindeer who was now standing on a tree stump, quivering.

'H-how long have you been here?' the reindeer asked in a worried little voice. His eyes darted about nervously.

'Oh,' said Winston, 'only a few minutes. I fell from the sky – well, from Hilda's back, really, but she was in the sky . . .' The reindeer now looked confused rather than terrified, so Winston started again, introducing himself and describing how Hilda had bumped her wing, causing him to tumble from her shoulders. 'Now I've lost her,' finished Winston. 'But I've found you!'

The reindeer relaxed, hopped down from the stump and trotted lightly across the snow to Winston. He was very young, and Winston found himself wondering why he was out here all alone in the middle of the night. Had he misplaced his mum too?

'I'm Jørgen,' said the reindeer, 'but everyone calls me Liten. It means *little*

and, well, I am quite small. Not as tiny as you, though.'

Winston had to agree with that. 'Have you seen my friend Hilda?' he asked. 'You can't mistake her – she's got a Christmas decoration on her head.'

Liten shook his head, but told Winston to come with him. Someone in his herd might have spotted her. 'I should be getting back anyway . . .' he said, looking around. Winston couldn't help but think that Liten was acting a little bit sheepish.

The pair ducked out from the small patch of woodland and on to the vast, frozen plains. The snow had stopped now and the night sky was clear and dark. In the distance the Northern Lights were dancing like ribbons among the stars.

The herd wasn't far away and they were all gathered around something, apparently greatly excited. Liten and Winston pushed through and found Hilda in the centre of things, ruffled and giddy, but thankfully all right. She'd obviously already made chums with her rescuers.

'AND HERE HE IS!' she cried in her loud voice. 'My friend I was telling you about. Not hurt, are you? I've bashed the old wing a bit, but it'll be OK with some rest. When this lovely lot found me, I was an absolute block of ice. Thankfully my dear new friend Gudrun sat on me for a bit to thaw me out, and here I am!' She pointed with her good wing at an enormous reindeer, who beamed.

Hilda continued talking loudly and at great speed, filling the herd in on her and Winston's adventure so far. 'We were heading north, you see,' she explained. 'In the hopes someone might recognize the words to Winston's song.' Using her good wing again, she pushed Winston into the centre of the herd. 'Go on,' she encouraged. 'Sing it!'

Winston suddenly felt very tired. There were lots of eyes on him and he'd been on the go for days now, only managing to snatch moments of sleep. Every bit of him, from his ears to the end of his tail, felt droopy. He felt that singing the song again was useless. No one had recognized the words so far, so why should this time be different? He kept getting excited that his mystery could be solved, but he was beginning to think it was hopeless.

He sighed, took a deep breath and sang the lullaby once more, his little voice ringing out across the vast, white, empty landscape. The reindeer listened carefully, but they all shook their heads. No one knew it.

Winston nodded sadly. It was what he had expected. 'Thank you anyway,' he said, with a brief smile. He felt cold and wanted to have a sleep.

But then Liten said, 'Wait a minute! Where's Mormor? She might know!'

Mormor, Liten explained, was his grandma.

'She knows lots of things,' continued Liten excitedly, 'all the old snow stories from the herd! She's like a living history book – if anyone can help you, I'm sure it will be her!'

Winston felt his heart start to thud wildly in his chest and his whiskers start to tremble. Could this be it? Could she finally be the one to recognize the lullaby?

Mormor was located a little way from the herd, fast asleep and snoring loudly. Liten galloped over and woke her up. She was very old and quite hard of hearing, so Liten had to explain three times what was happening before nudging Winston right over to his granny.

'Go on!' said Liten. 'Try it!'

Winston was even more nervous than before – Liten's grandma was his last hope.

Very slowly, trembling with anticipation, he clambered up on to Mormor's antlers so he was right by her ear. And as soon as he started singing, Mormor's face lit up. Her eyes sparkled.

'Know it?' she said. 'Of course I know it! My great-grandma used to sing it to me when I was a calf!'

Winston's heart drummed even faster. 'You . . . you know what language it is?' he whispered.

Mormor nodded her head, still smiling. 'Of course I do!' She twinkled. 'It's Old North Polish.'

Winston's heart drummed harder.

'My dear,' Mormor continued, 'I think you might have been born in the North Pole!'

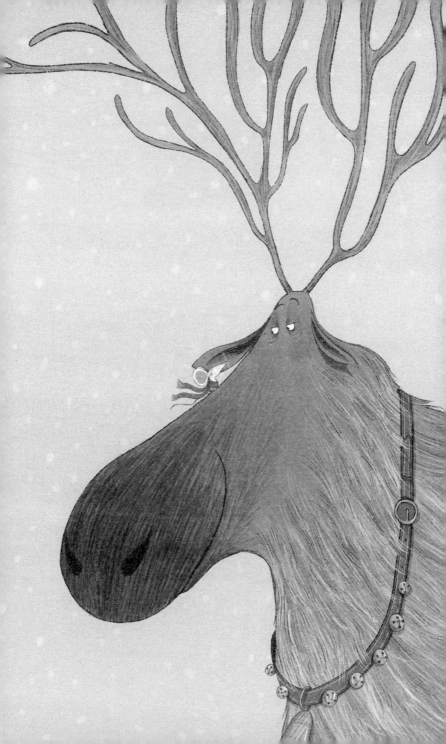

A VERY
OLD SONG

Winston shook his head to make sure that his ears were completely clear of ice and snow before asking Liten's grandmother to repeat what she'd just said.

'I think,' she said again in her deep,

gentle voice, 'that you might have been born in the North Pole!'

Winston couldn't believe it. He bubbled with questions. How? When? What? Mormor laughed, enjoying his giddy enthusiasm. She told him to sit down beside her and she would try to explain.

'I'm afraid I can't remember what all the words mean. It's been a very long time since I heard that song,' she said. 'But I know it mentions the North Star. It's that bright one there above us.'

Winston looked. Among all the other twinkling lights in the sky, one star shone the brightest. As he looked at it, that strange feeling in his chest appeared again, aching, but also now excited. He felt as if at least a little bit of the missing puzzle piece was slotting into place. He was from the North Pole! That's where he'd been born! Another wisp of memory floated through his head. He'd looked up at that star before, but that was a long time ago and he'd been looking at it through a window . . .

'It's a very old song and a beautiful one too. Whoever sang it to you must have loved you very much,' continued Mormor.

Winston nodded his head. He knew this was true. He could feel it in his heart. Despite the chill, a growing warmth was radiating from within him. He didn't know how all the other clues fitted – the rustling paper, the cooking smells, the scent of peppermint – but he knew without a doubt now that the North Pole held the answers.

'I need to get there!' he said. 'Hilda,

do you think you might be able to take me?'

Hilda looked down at her wing. It really was feeling very sore indeed. 'I don't think the wing is up to it tonight, old chum,' she said sadly. 'Let me rest the old flapper overnight and see how it is in the morning.'

Winston was desperate to leave right away, but he knew Hilda needed to rest. He didn't want her hurting herself even more than she had done. She'd already been terrifically kind, bringing him all this way, but Winston's heart was drumming in his chest and excitement was fizzing through him from nose to tail. He knew he HAD to get to the North Pole as soon as possible.

Winston thought very hard, and suddenly he had an idea. And it was a good one too.

'Can't reindeer fly?' he squeaked. 'Couldn't one of the herd here fly to the North Pole with me?'

But the reindeer shook their heads.

'No,' said Liten's father. 'Some reindeer fly, but the last one of our herd who could was Mormor's great-grandmother, and that was a long, long time ago now. None of us can do it, I'm afraid.'

Winston was so disappointed that his whiskers drooped.

'I think,' said Mormor kindly, 'you both need a good sleep. You'll stay with us for the night and in the morning we'll all try to think of a plan.' And so that was decided.

The herd all gathered around and huddled together. Winston and Hilda nestled down in the middle of them, amongst their soft, warm, furry bodies, and soon the owl was snoring away.

But Winston couldn't sleep. His mind was whirring. He was, he felt, within a whisker of solving his Very Curious Mystery and finding his mum, but it seemed that it would no longer happen. To make it worse, he wouldn't be able to get back to Oliver in time for Christmas either. This made Winston feel very sad indeed.

He sighed. The aching in his chest was back again, but this time it was worse than ever. He was miles from both of them and missed them dreadfully. Lying there all alone among the snoring herd, he wondered again how he'd managed to get himself from the North Pole to Mistletoe Street in the first place. It must have been something quite

extraordinary that had happened, but how strange that he now couldn't remember it . . .

He sighed again and, with his eyes prickling and every bit of him feeling crumpled and sad, he curled up into a tiny ball and went to sleep.

But it's amazing how quickly things can change.

A little while later, Winston woke up. In the darkness, someone was tapping him gently on the belly. He was too sleepy and sad to really open his eyes, so with a yawn he said, 'Yes? What is it?'

And then a voice whispered in his ear. It was a voice that quivered with excitement. It said: 'I've got something very important to tell you . . .'

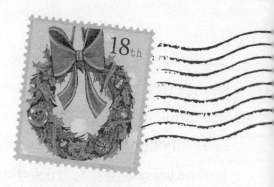

I'VE GOT SOMETHING VERY IMPORTANT TO TELL YOU

Winston's eyes pinged open and he looked around to find Liten standing beside him, holding a hoof up to his snout, telling him to keep quiet. Winston nodded and tapped Hilda, who was beside him, snoring. She woke with a start.

'Liten has something to tell us!' he whispered in his tiniest voice. Hilda's eyes widened.

'Follow me,' said Liten mysteriously, and he led them away from the sleeping herd towards the little patch of woodland where Winston had crash-landed earlier.

Winston's curiosity was such that he thought his whiskers would tie themselves in a knot. 'What is it, Liten?' he squeaked.

'It's a surprise!' the reindeer whispered.

Hilda and Winston looked at each other. What on earth was going on?

Liten hustled them under the branches and into the small clearing, then he suddenly stopped, looking shy and timid.

'Well, go on, then,' said Hilda, in her

gentle but bossy way. 'What's this Very Important Surprise?'

Liten looked around excitedly, and then said, 'I think I know how you can get to the North Pole.'

Winston's whiskers were trembling with anticipation now. 'How?' he said.

Liten closed his eyes. For a moment or two, nothing happened. Hilda and Winston glanced at each other again, both wondering if Liten had gone a bit bonkers.

But then something DID happen.

Something magical and extraordinary.

Every hair on Liten's body started to shimmer and glisten. He glittered from his tiny antlers to his stubby tail as if he'd been dipped in starlight. Suddenly, his nose began to glow. It turned from dark brown to yellow, to orange, to pink, to bright, holly-berry red. And then his hoofs gently lifted from the ground.

Liten opened his eyes. 'Am I doing it?' he cried. He looked down. 'I am! I'm doing it! I'm . . . I'm flying!'

And he was.

It was a very wobbly sort of flying, but he really was drifting through the chilly winter air. Leading with his glowing red nose, he did a slow loop round the clearing before landing with a tumble back on the ground.

'You can fly?' squeaked Winston, astounded.

Liten nodded. 'It . . . it started a few days ago. I sneezed, and I noticed my nose starting to glow. Then, before I knew it, I was floating with all my hoofs off the ground! It only happened for a split second, but I just knew I was flying. That's what I was doing earlier when you found me – I'd sneaked in here to make sure I hadn't been dreaming!'

'But why haven't you told your family?' asked Hilda, wide-eyed. 'I'm sure they'd be very excited!'

Liten looked sheepish. 'I will tell them,' he said, 'but, you see, it's usually only girl reindeer who have the ability to fly, and it doesn't happen until they are grown up. I must be a bit odd,' he finished, looking a bit glum.

Winston smiled at his friend. 'No, not odd,' he insisted. 'Special!'

Liten gave Winston a small smile back, then looked down at his hooves again. 'And everyone is always fussing over me,' he continued. 'They think because I'm tiny I can't do things. But I can! I can be brave! And . . . and I can take you to the North Pole! I know I can.'

'But you've only just learned to do it!' said Hilda. 'It's a long way to go to the North Pole on your own AND in all this snow. It might be very dangerous indeed! Winston, what do you think?'

Winston was quiet as he thought about it. Liten was certainly nowhere near as good at flying as Hilda, but at the same time Winston knew all about being tiny and how others could underestimate you just because of how you looked on the outside. He studied Liten and saw the same sparkle of fierce determination that he himself felt when he thought about his Very Curious Mystery.

'Let's do it!' he said, and Liten did an excited little hop around in a circle.

Hilda still looked worried, but could see how important it all was to Winston. She gave him a hug with her good wing and helped him climb up on to Liten's still-glittering back. 'I'll tell your family in the morning,' Hilda said to Liten. 'Just the pair of you be jolly careful, all right?'

Winston and Liten nodded solemnly and listened carefully as Hilda told them she thought they would need a good run-up for their flight. She led them out to the other side of the little woodland so they were still hidden from the herd. In front of them, for as far as the eye could see, were the seemingly endless, empty, snow-covered plains.

'Ready?' said Liten.

Winston nestled down deeper into his friend's fur and gripped on as tightly as he could with his paws. 'Ready!' he squeaked. With a nod to Hilda, Liten started to run.

Faster and faster he galloped, a fine

white powdery trail of snow kicking up behind him. The moonlight shone as his fur glittered wildly, the sparkles dancing and fizzing with magic. His nose glowed again, berry red and as bright and as shiny as a lantern.

'Here we go!' he cried, and Winston gripped on even tighter.

Then with a leap Liten flung himself into the air, and within moments he and Winston were climbing steeply through the star-spangled sky.

FIRST FLIGHT

Higher and higher Winston and Liten climbed. The air was crisp and clear and freezing cold, and the wind whipping around Winston made his eyes water but his heart soar.

The flight was more than a little

wobbly at first. It took Liten quite a while to get his limbs going in the right direction and all working at the same time. Great foggy clouds of breath bloomed in front of the little reindeer's nose with the effort as his legs galloped through the sky.

Carefully, Winston crept closer to his new friend's ears and called and hollered encouragement over the noise of the air streaming by them. The pair flew through curtains of clouds and patches of tumbling snow, but for the most part the sky was open and vast.

The higher Liten flew, the colder it got. In the distance, stars shone, the moon glowed and the Northern Lights danced in waves in front of them. At one point, Winston thought he saw a shooting star –

it was definitely something hurtling through the sky at speed – but he was too busy watching for the North Star to pay it much attention. Liten's grandma had said the lullaby mentioned it, and he was sure it would take them to the North Pole and hopefully straight to Winston's mum.

A sudden shiver of cold air made Winston's whiskers tingle, snapping him from his thoughts. He looked about, but everything was now a jumble of snowflakes and thick clouds. The clear night sky had disappeared and, Winston realized, so had the North Star.

'We've hit a snowstorm!' shouted Liten over the wind. 'It's going to be a bit bumpy!' As if on cue, the wind buffeted against the little reindeer, and on his back Winston had to grip on for dear life.

'Do you know where we are?' called Winston.

'No!' said Liten. Then, 'Yes! No! I'm not sure!'

'What do you mean?' cried Winston.

'Well, I don't know where I am but . . . but I think my nose does!' shouted Liten.

Winston looked at Liten's snout. It was still glowing, illuminating a small patch of the clouds around them, but it was now also flashing.

'And it seems to be telling my legs where to go!' continued Liten excitedly.

Winston watched in amazement as Liten's nose swung to the side, pulling his whole body with it. Beneath him, the reindeer's legs pulled powerfully through the clouds and then suddenly burst through them.

'I THINK WE ARE ABOUT TO LAND!' cried Liten.

Winston only just had time to tighten his paws round Liten's fur before – WALLOP!

They hit the ground, tumbling over and over themselves in thick, powdery snow.

Winston sat up and cleared the ice from his eyelashes. He gasped.

In front of them was a large, old, snow-covered house.

And in a window a light was flickering.

LOST

'Where are we?' whispered Liten, picking himself up and shaking off the thick coat of snow his bumpy landing had dressed him in.

'I don't know . . .' said Winston, then he shook his head. No, that wasn't quite right. Although he was sure he hadn't been in this place before, he seemed to know exactly where he was. 'Actually – I do know!' he continued excitedly. 'This is Mince Pie House! This is the home of Father Christmas!'

Liten's eyes widened as he looked around. 'Those must be the reindeer stables!' he said, nodding his little antlers in the direction of a wooden building covered thickly in snow. 'Where the famous flying reindeer live!' His tail wagged excitedly, and Winston could see that his friend was desperate to go and investigate.

'Go on!' he said. 'I'm going to go in there.' Winston pointed at the house.

Liten galloped off, and Winston was left all alone. He was feeling a little bit peculiar. After travelling all this way, all those miles, was his mum on the other side of the door? He felt excited and nervous all at the same time.

But then he realized that another strange sensation was jingling through his little body. It was as if he wasn't quite in control of himself. He looked down in surprise to see his feet walking softly over the snow towards the entrance. Then he watched in a daze as his paw lifted and he hammered on the thick wooden front door. He seemed to be doing everything automatically, as if something else was directing him. Was it magic?

KNOCK! KNOCK!

No one answered.

Winston tried again, but the wind was howling around the building, and he was very small, so his tiny knocks were snatched away by the blizzard. He looked around for another way in and spotted a gap under the door.

Just where I knew it would be . . . he thought, amazed. With a heave and a POP! Winston was soon inside.

It was warm in the hallway, so toasty after Winston's midnight dash through the snowy night sky, and although it was dimly lit, with the lights turned down low, the place was cheerful and cosy. Winston found himself padding down the corridor, running a paw against the walls. The wallpaper was an intricate design of holly leaves and berries and ribbons and little parcels.

'I've seen this before . . .' he whispered.

Soon Winston came to a door, which opened out into an enormous workshop. The space seemed too big to fit into the house he'd looked at from outside and, once again, Winston wondered if there was magic at work in this place. Everywhere he looked there were large, high desks with teetering stools beside them. Shelves stacked with boxes reached high up into the ceiling and tall, wobbly-looking ladders were balancing precariously here and there. The room was, Winston had to admit, very untidy. Spools of ribbons had unravelled all over the place and the floor was littered with the tiny snippings of wrapping paper.

It was also completely empty.

Winston frowned. He didn't know how he knew, but he was sure that this wasn't right.

'This room should be bustling!' he said, and, squinting, he allowed his mind to fill it with imaginary helpers all busying about and excited. Yes, that's exactly what should have been happening here. He opened his eyes fully and rubbed his nose thoughtfully. Where were they all?

He decided to look for clues and scampered about, not really knowing what he was searching for. Then he spotted something interesting.

On one of the desks was a very important-looking clipboard that held a sheet of paper. It was a calendar showing all the days in December. Most of the dates were crossed off with an X, but they stopped on the box marked the twenty-fourth.

Winston gasped and he started to feel a bit hot about the ears. 'Today is CHRISTMAS EVE?' he squeaked. He suddenly understood why the place was so empty and quiet. All the busy helpers who should have been there were tucked up in bed. All the presents for Father Christmas's sleigh were packed up and ready to be delivered. Their work was finished.

Winston sat down with a flump. His whiskers drooped.

I'm too late! he thought. *I've come all this way looking for an answer and I'm too late. No one is here who can help me and I'm miles and miles and miles away from Oliver! I PROMISED I'd be back for Christmas and I won't be.*

Winston's eyes began to prickle. He was a very brave mouse, but right at that moment he didn't feel brave at all.

'What am I going to do?' he said to himself, his little voice echoing around the enormous, empty room. He'd been so sure that he was on the right track to solve his mystery. Everything was pointing to this place and he still had that strange feeling of knowing where he was, or at least half remembering it. And yet all the clues didn't make sense. This room didn't smell of any of the things he'd remembered. There were wafts of sticky tape and wrapping paper here instead of cooking smells and peppermint.

Winston's tail quivered with worry. On the rest of his adventure he'd always found a new friend who had helped him on his way, but now there was nobody. He felt very tired and lost and tiny.

He realized then that he was shivering, although it wasn't cold in the workshop. A little draught was whispering into the room from somewhere – somewhere nearby – and it was making his fur dance. He found himself drying his eyes with his scarf as once again that feeling of being led by something invisible took over him. He stood up and allowed his feet to lead him towards where the draught was coming from.

There was another door.

His mum's voice came to him then, singing the lullaby. His whiskers wobbled and his nose twitched as he smelt something on the breeze coming from the next room.

It was the exact warm, gingery, biscuity smell he had remembered. And then, more faintly but still there, peppermint.

'I AM in the right place,' Winston whispered. He hardly dared to believe it. Was his mum just on the other side of the door?

And so, with his heart leaping with anticipation and his whiskers dancing, Winston clambered under the door.

FOUND?

Winston found himself in another hallway, with two rooms leading off from it. Once again being led by either his memories or the strange winter magic that was tingling in the air, he wandered towards the closest room.

There was a sign on the door.

TEA-BREAK STATION

Yes, thought Winston, *just as I thought.* Then he shook his head. *No, not thought – remembered.*

He entered the room, taking it all in. The gigantic, many-spouted teapot wrapped up in a brightly coloured tea cosy, the wall with hundreds of mugs hanging from little hooks, the enormous biscuit tin sitting on the table.

Winston clambered up to it and, with a little bit of huffing and puffing, he managed to heave the lid off it. He sniffed, and his nose and whiskers twitched with joy. This was exactly the smell he'd remembered. It was rich and spicy, with a crisp little tingle of frost at the edge of it.

Ice ginger!

That's what it was. Gingerbread, but made with ice ginger, which had grown outside in the snow. He saw the knobbly, icy root in his mind's eye and remembered that it could only be grown at the North Pole.

Winston's belly rumbled. He realized he hadn't eaten for a very long time and he was famished. He didn't suppose the owner of the tin would mind if he had just a little nibble, so he reached in, snapped a bit off one of the cookies and bit into it. It was whisker-wobblingly delicious.

Was I born here? he wondered. *In this little kitchen?* The biscuit smell was right, but what of the other clues? The flickering

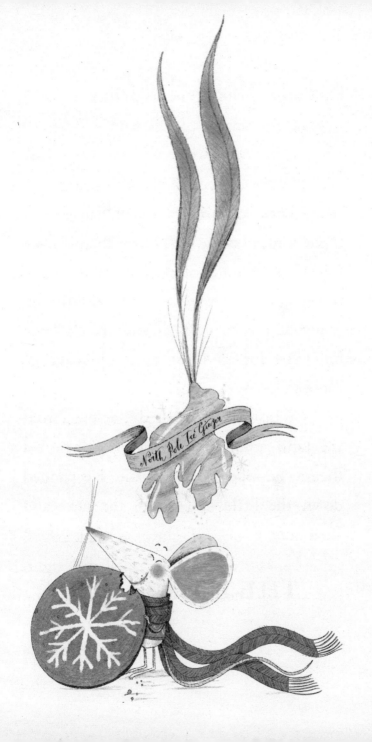

light, the rustling noise and the smell of peppermint?

Winston looked around. No, this wasn't the right place.

Then he sniffed. He caught that faint smell of peppermint again, and then his ears swivelled this way and that. He'd heard something. A voice. Someone was humming. Someone was humming the tune he'd been following for all those days and over all those miles.

Winston clambered down from the table and, as if he was floating in a dream, he followed the music. He padded down the little hallway to the next and final door.

THE POST ROOM

With all the effort he could muster, Winston pushed at the heavy door and it opened just enough for him to squeeze inside.

He gasped.

He was exactly where he'd been visiting in his memories. This room was so familiar to him. The enormous old desk in front of a window through which he could see thick snowflakes falling silently in the moonlight. The piles of letters and envelopes. The endless scrolls of lists, all checked twice. The boxes full of paper teetering in great towers all around the place and the large, thick sacks lined up wherever there was space.

Winston breathed in. *Yes*, he thought, *everything fits*. The dry, papery smell hadn't been from books, but from letters and envelopes. Hundreds of them – no, THOUSANDS of them – arriving from all over the world to this little room where they were read and enjoyed, their contents noted down. Then, when Christmas Eve approached, parcels were brought in by the sackful to be

checked before being loaded on to a sleigh.

And there, just visible from where he was standing on the floor, was the flickering light of a lantern, and a jar on the desk filled to bursting with striped peppermint candy canes for the letter reader to snack on while they studied each note carefully.

Winston's feet started to lead him towards the desk where, carefully, he started to clamber up the over-stuffed drawers. His heart was drumming as the sound of the gentle humming grew louder in his ears.

The surface of the desk was incredibly untidy. He picked his way around pencil shavings and piles of envelopes, almost tripping over a length of striped string, his eyes darting around for any sign of whoever was humming. Soon he came to a tall pile of papers and, behind them, just visible above the clutter, was a typewriter. Behind the machine he found a row of little mouse beds, each made from empty matchboxes or old tins of jelly beans or paperclips. They were all empty.

Then he stopped suddenly. He'd been so busy looking and remembering that he hadn't realized the humming had stopped. All was silent.

And then there was a voice. 'Winston?'

Winston spun round. In front of the window, their faces lit by the warm, cosy light of a candle, were five mice. Five mice Winston found himself recognizing. There was a series of names suddenly dancing on the tip of his tongue.

'Wilfred and Walter and William and Winnabelle and Wilhelmina,' he whispered.

They looked at each other.

'You're my brothers and sisters, aren't you?' said Winston. The other mice nodded. Their whiskers jangled with joy and all their ears turned bright pink with delight.

Winston stumbled backwards. And, suddenly, everything became clear.

THE FOG CLEARS

Winston sat down heavily, blinking in amazement.

In his mind, the wobbly, foggy haziness of his memories slowly cleared. Suddenly he knew what had happened all that time ago in this room. It was coming back to him in flashes and swirls. Winston closed his eyes and tried to get it all in order, to sort it tidily like he did with the post at the Mistletoe Street toy shop.

The post.

Of course. It had all started with the post – the post in this cosy, untidy, little mail room. The place where generations of Winston's ancestors had lived, warm among the papers, helping to sort Father Christmas's post.

It's no wonder I'm good at helping Oliver with it all, thought Winston with a smile. *I was born surrounded by letters and parcels!*

He was in his memories once again, but this time they were crystal clear and Winston felt like a secret snooper watching his rememberings as they danced in his head.

He saw the desk very much as it was now, cluttered with papers and letters. He smelt all the familiar smells, he saw the lantern with the candle flickering inside. But instead of being there alone he could see six tiny little mouselings, his brothers and sisters, all tucked up and asleep. And there, right at the end, so teeny and snug in his little matchbox bed, he saw himself. His younger self was, he noted, wide awake.

Just then, still in his memories, he saw his mum appear. She had a piece of string caught on her tail and Winston remembered how at night, when everyone was asleep, she would go and help sort the post ready for the morning. He watched as she busied over to her mouselings to check on them.

'Goodness me, Winston!' she said when

she got to his younger self. 'What are you doing still awake?'

Tiny Winston said that he just couldn't get to sleep.

'Oh dear,' she said. 'We know how to fix that, don't we? Come on, Little Whiskers.' She picked him up out of his bed and carried him past his sleeping siblings over to the lantern in the window. Snow was gently drifting past outside and the North Star was shining like a diamond.

'Our special star,' she said, then she started to rock him gently and began singing the lullaby in her quiet, gentle voice. This time, Winston could understand the words perfectly.

The snow has come, soft and white,
glittering, glistening
under the North Star's light.

Hush, little mouseling, close your eyes.
It's late.
It's time for bed.
It's time to say goodnight.

But don't you worry, don't fret,
Go to sleep,
And I'll be here
Always holding you, holding you tight.

'Now it really is time for bed,' said his mum softly, and he followed as she put Tiny Winston into his matchbox. She lay beside him, stroking his nose gently. She yawned, and it wasn't long before Winston noticed her drifting off to sleep.

But Little Winston was still awake. His stomach rumbled.

'I was hungry!' Winston whispered to himself, and he chuckled. 'I am always hungry!'

Tiny Winston sat up slowly, careful not wake anyone, and Winston found himself remembering this exact moment. He remembered that grumbling feeling in his stomach and how an idea had formed in his head. He'd decided to sneak off to the little tea-break room next door to help himself to an ice ginger biscuit. He remembered thinking how happy his mum would be the next morning when she found he had brought one back for her – they were her favourites, after all.

Winston watched as his younger self, obviously delighted with his Very Important Plan, climbed out of bed and tiptoed across the desk, giggling with excitement. It must have been very close to Christmas, as the room was even more cramped and untidy than usual, with sacks of presents waiting to be loaded on to the sleigh.

The lantern light was very low now, and with a fizz the candle inside extinguished. The room was suddenly much darker. Winston observed, his heartbeat quickening as his tiny younger self stood wobbling at the edge of the desk. It was a long way to the floor and the drawers were closed, so there wasn't even a makeshift staircase to help him down. Tiny Winston scratched his head, thinking, then he spotted a length of string.

He grabbed it and tied it to one of the candy canes. Then he started to climb down over the edge of the desk. But his paws were little and the knot he'd tied wasn't very strong, so it unravelled and –

BUMP!

Winston opened his eyes and found himself back in the real world with his brothers and sisters sitting beside him.

'I went to get a biscuit and fell . . .
I . . . I must have bumped my head,' he said
slowly. 'I must have accidentally fallen into
a sack and then it was put on the sleigh
and . . . and that's how I ended up miles
away from here!'

His siblings all hugged him tightly.
'We've spent such a long time wondering
what happened,' said Wilfred. 'We thought
you must have ended up with the parcels,
but we didn't know where you might be –
you could have been anywhere in the world!'

'But now I'm back!' said Winston
excitedly, his heart drumming with delight.
Memories of his brothers and sisters were
flooding back to him, as if he'd never been
away. He remembered how William and
Wilhelmina always finished each other's

sentences and how Walter hiccupped when he got excited and how Winnabelle hugged her tail close to her chest when she was listening to a story very carefully. It was so marvellous to be back with his family. But, he realized, someone was still missing. Two people in fact.

'Where's our mum?' he said. He was desperate to see her and to tell her all about his exciting adventures. 'And . . . there should be another one of us . . .' He searched for the name – *Winsome*. His big sister Winsome, who snorted when she laughed.

Wilfred was all of a fluster. 'Well,' he said, 'you see, Mum found a clue. There was a letter, and the boy who wrote it mentioned a mouse named Winston and a doll's house . . .'

Winnabelle rustled about in a pile and pulled out a scrap of paper. Winston recognized Oliver's writing.

William started gabbling. 'There was something about a toy shop and a Mistletoe Street and—'

'We think she's gone to find you!' finished Wilhelmina.

'We woke up a few days ago and she'd gone,' squeaked Winnabelle.

'There was a note on the typewriter saying "I will come home",' said Walter.

Winston couldn't believe it. He'd been looking for his mum and she had been looking for him. His mum hadn't forgotten him at all – she'd wanted to find him so badly that she'd set off alone all the way from the North Pole! She was on her way to

Mistletoe Street at this very moment!

Who knows? thought Winston excitedly. *She might even be there already!* And he imagined her tucking Oliver into bed, and it made him grin.

'Winsome went to find her. A Very Important Rescue Mission. She sneaked on to Father Christmas's sleigh and took off with that,' said William.

'We have to catch up with her!' squeaked Winston. 'And then find Mum!'

'We can't,' said Wilfred. 'There's no way to reach her – all the reindeer have gone.'

Winston groaned and sat down gloomily on the edge of the lantern. He remembered the shooting star he'd seen earlier while riding on Liten's back and wondered if maybe, just maybe, that had actually been the sleigh. Just his luck to have solved his Very Curious Mystery only to find that his mum wasn't there AND he was too late to get home for Christmas morning.

But then he remembered something. It made him leap to his feet.

He was so excited his whiskers were wobbling about like billy-o.

'Not all the reindeer have left!' he squeaked.

FOLLOW
THAT SLEIGH

Everything happened very quickly. Winston and his siblings clambered down from the desk and raced from the room. Down the corridor they went, past the tea-break room, back through the silent workshop, down the hall and, with a squeeze and a wiggle, out under the door and into the snow-covered courtyard outside.

It was really terribly cold out there now, especially after being in the cosy warmth of Father Christmas's house. It was also rather difficult to see anything through the thickly falling snow.

'Where's this reindeer friend of yours?' asked Walter, shivering.

Before Winston could answer, Liten came bounding round the corner from the stable block.

'Oh, there you are!' he cried. 'Oh! There are lots of you now!' He held out a hoof and politely shook paws with Winston's family. 'I wondered where you'd gone,' he continued. 'There wasn't a single reindeer in the stables at all. There were lots of nice warm-looking beds and an entire wall FULL of medals from the Reindeer Games, but no reindeer!'

Rapidly, and in very squeaky, excitable voices, Winston and his brothers and sisters explained everything to Liten – that it was actually Christmas Eve right this very moment, that Winston's mum had gone to find him and how they desperately needed to catch up with their sister who was on Father Christmas's sleigh.

As he listened, Liten's eyes widened and his eyebrows waggled. The clouds of warm breath billowing from his nose into the frosty, frozen air came in short, excited bursts so that he looked like a steam train, huffing and puffing.

'Do you think you can do it?' asked Winston hurriedly. 'You aren't too tired from flying earlier?'

Liten struck a particularly gallant and brave-looking pose. 'I LAUGH IN THE FACE OF TIREDNESS!' he cried. Then he bowed magnificently to allow Wilfred and Walter and William and Winnabelle and Wilhelmina and Winston to climb on to his back.

'Are you sure about this?' whispered Wilfred nervously.

'Not really,' said Winston matter-of-factly. 'But with adventures, you sometimes just need to get cracking and believe everything will work out OK.' Then he leaned forward and cried, 'FOLLOW THAT SLEIGH!'

Liten's fur started to glisten once again with its magical, shimmering glow. The mice held on tightly as he began to gallop. Faster and faster across the snow he went, his hoofs beating like a drum against the ice, and then with a terrific leap he took to the air.

It was much smoother this time. Liten swooped and climbed and soared through the sky like he was meant to be there. He burst through the snow clouds and into the vast, velvet sky beyond. The North Star shone behind them and in the distance the moon glowed like an enormous golden chocolate coin.

'The sleigh could be anywhere!' Winnabelle squeaked loudly into Winston's ear above the noise of the roaring wind. 'How will we ever find it?'

Winston grinned. 'Don't worry!' he cried. 'Liten's nose!'

'Liten knows what?' said Wilfred.

'No!' said Winston. 'His NOSE! I think it might be leading us to the sleigh!'

And indeed it was. It had started to glow

bright, holly-berry red again and soon it was in charge of Liten entirely. They swooped back under the snow clouds and raced through the blizzard. Black, churning seas and steep cliffs whipped by beneath them, then tall, frozen mountains and towns and cities, fields and gardens, palaces and apartment blocks.

Then Winston spotted something in the distance. 'Look!' he cried. 'Over there!'

'Can you reach it?' called Winston to Liten.

Liten nodded. He'd try his very best – Winston was depending on him.

It was hard work, though. The sleigh had an entire herd of fully grown, prize-winning reindeer pulling it, and they were going at a simply astonishing pelt. Poor Liten's small legs had to work double – no, triple speed to even attempt to catch up. But he did it. Before long he was cantering through the sky in line with the overflowing sacks in the back of the sleigh.

As they drew close, Winston and his siblings started to shout. 'Winsome! WINSOME!' And a moment later a small mousey face popped up from within a pile of parcels. She waved wildly and grinned with delight when she spotted Winston.

But the blizzard blowing about them had intensified. The snow was falling in thick, heavy sheets and the wind was blowing Liten this way and that as he tried to keep up with the speed of the sleigh.

'I think I'll have to slow down,' panted Liten. He looked and sounded exhausted. 'You'll have to jump on to the sleigh!'

Winston nodded, but his siblings squeaked in alarm. Far below them, the ground was racing by at a tremendous speed! The buildings and trees looked minute, even tinier than the furniture of a doll's house.

But Winston was a Mouse of Great Determination. Extremely carefully, he pulled himself up to standing. The wind swirled around him, and he wobbled. His ears flapped and his tail and scarf whipped about, snapping against the air. He helped his brothers and sisters to their feet. They all held tightly to each other's paws.

'Trust me!' Winston whispered, and they all nodded. Then, as the sleigh sailed past the bright December moon, the mice took deep breaths, closed their eyes and . . .

JUMPED.

I'VE MISSED YOU

The sleigh landed on the icy ground of Mistletoe Street with a bump before gently coming to a stop. The blizzard had blown over and now the snow was falling softly like icing sugar on a cake, and the street itself had never looked lovelier.

The hodge-podge roofs of buildings were too much of a jumble for Father Christmas to land safely upon, so instead he parked his sleigh at the bottom of the hill in the little park by the frozen duck pond, and began delivering his presents.

During the flight, Winston had giggled when he'd heard Father Christmas exclaim, 'Goodness! Where have you come from?' as Liten had landed with a bit of a clatter beside him at the front of the sleigh. Once Liten had caught his breath, he'd swooped excitedly around the flying herd with his nose glowing. The reindeer had bowed their antlers to the visitor and insisted that he join them.

With Father Christmas's back turned, Winston and his siblings emerged from one of the enormous sacks of presents.

'Do you think she'll have made it here yet?' asked Wilfred anxiously. 'It's a long way for her to have travelled on her own and anything could have happened on her journey!'

Winston agreed that this was true, but something within him told him that if anyone could do it, it was his mum. He must have got his adventurous spirit from someone, after all.

The air was tingling with Christmas magic and despite the cold Winston felt a warmth glowing inside him.

He led his mouse family out of the little park and on to the street. In the distance, the cathedral bells were chiming. The snow was falling gently over the sleeping buildings, and the shop windows were glowing brightly like jewels in the darkness. The night smelt of frost mingled with the warming smell of the smoke dancing in ribbons from all the higgledy chimney pots.

Winston hadn't walked far when he noticed footprints in the snow. Tiny MOUSE footprints.

'She's here!' Winston whispered. He felt that curious sensation in his chest, the one that had led him on his journey, and it was urging him on again. *It's like Liten's nose*, thought Winston to himself. *It's leading me right to where I need to be!*

The footsteps led up the hill of Mistletoe Street towards the toy shop, and Winston and his siblings followed them. It was a steep climb for tiny paws, and especially for Winston. His paws were the smallest and he was feeling tired. It had been a long few days and he'd slept so little, but he was excited too. It wiggled about inside him now, dancing around with a flicker of nerves. What would he say when he saw his mum again?

He heard the bells begin to chime a different tune. It was his tune – his mum's special lullaby.

Winston's heart hammered in his chest. He started to run. He left his siblings to follow him as he raced up the street, his paws stitching a little line of pawprints beside his mother's and his scarf flying wildly out behind him.

The road wiggled round one corner and then another and then . . .

The toy-shop window, with

his beautiful doll's-house home in the centre of it, was lit up, its warm yellowy-orange glow so cosy against the cold night.

And there she was.

In the street below, looking up at the sparkling display, was a little mouse, all bundled up against the chill and silhouetted against the light.

It was his mum.

Winston walked towards her slowly as the lullaby rang out around them.

She turned.

For a moment, Winston and his mum just looked at each other. All was quiet except for the sound of Winston's heart beating in his little chest. He took everything in: their matching velvet noses, their matching pink cheeks.

There was so much to be said – important things – but where to start? Should he tell her about how he got lost? Or about the adventures he'd been on to find her? About his adventure that had criss-crossed this way and that across the world?

No.

In the end, Winston realized that sometimes, at moments like this when there is a lot to say, the best thing to do is to actually say nothing at all.

So instead they ran to each other, their paws pattering across the snow and their arms outstretched, and they squeezed each other in the tightest hug you can ever imagine.

It was the type of hug that said the only thing that was really important.

It said, 'I've missed you.'

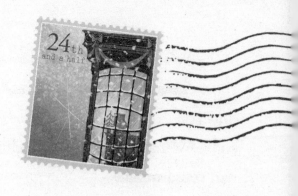

HOME

Christmas Day that year was a very loud and exciting affair. Winston, his mum and his siblings nattered all night in the warmth of Winston's doll's-house home. They chattered and laughed and sang and really had the most wonderful time.

When Oliver came running down the stairs the next morning, he couldn't believe his eyes.

'Winston!' he cried. 'You're home! You said you'd come back – you promised and you did! And you've . . . you've brought friends!'

Winston squeaked with delight as he introduced his human family to his mouse family. He very proudly took one of Oliver's fingers and pulled him over to shake paws with each of his brothers and sisters, and finally with his mum. The giddiness and excitement were overwhelming and Oliver's parents had to take themselves into the kitchen for a hot cup of tea to give their ears a rest.

But the excitement and surprises didn't finish there.

Despite the shop being closed for the day, the front doorbell didn't stop jangling. Oliver watched in amazement as visitor after visitor arrived, each more extraordinary than the next.

First came an exquisitely fluffy white cat wearing the most enormous diamond collar anyone had ever seen. On her back was a rat, resplendent in velvet, with his hat tilted rakishly on his head.

Next there came a large pigeon and an almost completely spherical robin who seemed to be only half awake. An elderly bat then arrived, and they all hopped merrily into the shop and joined the party in the window.

Then, later, came an astounding appearance that made Oliver rub his eyes to make sure he really was seeing what was in front of him. Just after breakfast, a lilac poodle trotted into the shop. At some point recently, he'd obviously been a very well-trimmed, clipped and pampered pooch, but now he was looking utterly windswept and thoroughly pleased about that too. He had with him a large collection of mice who paraded into the toy shop carrying an array of delicious-smelling baked goods in their paws.

'But all the bakeries are closed today...' muttered Oliver's mum from the doorstep.

And, just as everyone was about to settle down for a delicious Christmas feast, the doorbell went again. On the doorstep, sitting very neatly indeed, was a fox. And on his head was a rat wrapped in a beautiful shawl. Behind them was a rather tired-looking owl with a string of popcorn round her neck. She was wearing a Christmas decoration on her head and appeared to be delighted by the smell of food wafting from the kitchen.

By bedtime, Oliver was completely bamboozled by it all. He had to have his bedtime story downstairs in the shop as there was no room on his bed for all the new arrivals to join him there. As he took himself back up to his attic bedroom, Oliver's mind was tripping giddily over itself with questions. Where had Winston been? Who were these visitors and where had they come from? Had the extraordinary events of the day been real?

Downstairs, Winston was also

marvelling at everything. Here was his family, all together under one roof – the ones who looked like him and the ones who didn't, but who were family all the same. He loved each and every one of them, and they loved him.

And it was then he realized that the strange aching feeling in his chest, the empty one that felt like a missing jigsaw piece, had vanished, and in its place was something new. It was a happy, full, warm and lovely feeling that felt like the hug his mum had given him outside in the snow. Winston knew then that this new feeling would stay with him always.

And if Oliver had peeked out of his window at midnight, he would have seen a tiny reindeer, its fur shimmering like starlight, pay a flying visit to the shop. He would have wondered again if his eyes were playing tricks on him, but they wouldn't have been. The reindeer really was there, dancing in the falling snow with Winston and his family.

Because that's the thing about Christmas – the thing you must always remember: magic fizzes in the air, and very strange and wonderful things really can and do happen.

Even if you are a mouse.

The End

Hello!

I've always loved winter. All those frosty mornings and getting cosy after being outside in the cold. And when December arrives Christmas magic is in the air!

The busy bustling shops, the glitzy decorations, the waiting and then of course the big day itself!

I got the idea when I was helping my niece and nephews write their letters to Father Christmas and I wondered (with a shiver) what would happen if one of the letters got waylaid? Hopefully there would be some kind person (or in this case a mouse) to deliver it for us. And what adventures would they have?

Of course Christmas isn't just about the things you buy from the shops. I wanted to write a story about

A Christmas angel
I made aged 4!
(He's very old now!)

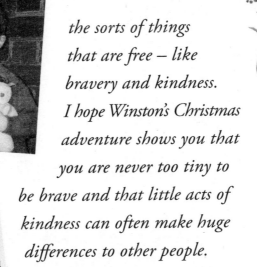

the sorts of things
that are free – like
bravery and kindness.
I hope Winston's Christmas
adventure shows you that
you are never too tiny to
be brave and that little acts of
kindness can often make huge
differences to other people.

I hope you've enjoyed this
book and that you might come
back to it next year and share it
with other people in your family
and with friends.

Have a very cosy
Christmas and an
adventurous New Year!

love from Alex
x

← Me, aged two, playing in the snow!

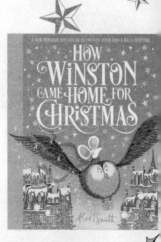

A THRILLING FESTIVE ADVENTURE

HOW WINSTON DELIVERED CHRISTMAS

To Father Christmas
Mince Pie House

Alex T Smith

Alex T Smith

THE TWELVE DAYS OF CHRISTMAS

or

Grandma is Overly Generous

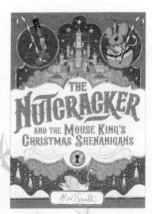

THE NUTCRACKER

AND THE MOUSE KING'S CHRISTMAS SHENANIGANS

Alex T Smith

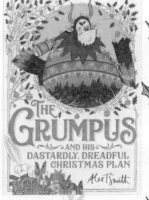

THE GRUMPUS

AND HIS DASTARDLY, DREADFUL CHRISTMAS PLAN

Alex T Smith

ALEX T. SMITH
is the creator of
bestselling festive
favourites *How Winston
Delivered Christmas*,
*How Winston Came
Home for Christmas*, *The Grumpus* and the
witty retellings of *The Nutcracker* and *The
Twelve Days of Christmas*, which are all set to
become future Christmas classics. He is also
the creator of the Claude series and the Astrid
and the Space Cadets series for early readers.

Alex lives in the UK, under the watchful
eye of his small canine companions and
a flock of unruly chickens.